Love on the Links

Romancing the Dog series

Love on the Links

Romancing the Dog series

One of three romance novellas
by
Marjorie Pinkerton Miller

SUNACUMEN
PRESS
Colorado Springs, CO

Sunacumen Press
Colorado Springs, CO

Second Edition

Cover art by vanda_g/istock.com
Cover design, interior formatting by Sunacumen Press

ISBN: 979-8-9914967-4-2

Printed in the United States of America

To Chrissy Meyer, the world's best beta-reader

One

WHAT BETH LOVED MOST ABOUT her fifth-floor condo in Seattle was the view of Puget Sound she had from its west-facing balcony. Yes, there were a few warm days when she wished the evening sun didn't shine directly through the big sliders into the living room, but no one in Seattle ever complained about getting too much sun.

She appreciated the balcony for another reason: Chi-Chi. The big dog loved the sun, and every chance she could get, she lay out there, soaking up the heat of the rays. If Chi-Chi could have spent all her daylight hours on the balcony, she surely would have. Luckily, the malamute mix wasn't a barker, and Beth let her out whenever she was home, although the dog preferred Beth's big queen bed once the sun set.

None of this made Dan happy, however. He would have preferred ChiChi live somewhere else entirely, and it was partly because of their canine disconnect that Beth kept brushing off Dan's insistence on setting a date for their wedding.

On the balcony one summer evening, Beth pulled her feet out from under ChiChi's shaggy body and drained the last of the wine from her glass. She picked up the bottle she and Dan had just finished and stood.

"I'm going to start making dinner." She pulled the sliding glass door open. ChiChi looked up for a moment before deciding to stay right where she was, even if it meant sharing the balcony with Dan. Her big head plopped back down, and she sighed audibly.

"But we're not done with this conversation," Dan argued. "I really want to make a decision now."

"I'm not ready to set a date," Beth answered. She fell back down on her chair and slumped forward.

"You love me. You want to get married. Right?"

"Sure." Beth moved her head up and down, but it wasn't a convincing nod. "I think. I just don't understand why we have to decide this now."

Dan looked at her with a long face, his eyelids drooping as if he were exhausted. "You know what the problem is?" he asked. He didn't wait for her answer. "We love each other, but we don't have enough in common. I love golf and you love dogs. Your friends are bohemians and canines, and mine are married grown-ups with kids. I think what we need is to develop a mutual passion."

Beth couldn't disagree, but as she stared at the reflection of the setting sun rippling across the sound, she couldn't imagine what mutual passion—or even mutual like—they could develop at this point in their three-year relationship.

"That makes sense, I suppose," she said. "But that isn't going to help me get dinner ready tonight." She pushed herself back up out of her chair, but Dan reached over and put a hand on her arm to stop her.

"I think you should learn to play golf," he said. He

reached into a rear pocket and pulled out what looked like a brochure—folded in half to fit alongside his billfold. He unfolded it and studied it like he'd never seen it before.

"Right. And I think you should learn to love dogs," Beth answered.

"That's not going to happen," he said, continuing to peruse the brochure in his hand. "Once ChiChi is adopted, I don't want you to get another one."

"I'm not promising that. I've never lived without a dog. I would own one instead of just fostering if I weren't trying to make you happy."

"Okay, we'll cross that bridge … ." Dan stopped. His voice had started to rise as it always did when the topic of Beth's canine obsessions was raised. He lowered it. "But how about golf?"

"I'm no good at it," Beth said flatly, remembering their disastrous outings to the driving range and the course the summer before. "And when you try to teach me, we always end up fighting."

"That's why I think we should do this." Dan tossed the brochure in front of her.

Beth looked at the front of the colorful trifold. Three gorgeous women stood in a line, each holding a golf club as if ready to swing, smiling big, toothy grins. In front of them, clearly endangering his life by standing there, a man held up his arms as if demonstrating some immutable physical law that controlled the universe—or perhaps just the perfect golf swing.

A smart trick, Beth thought: showing women, not men learning to play golf. This brochure was designed with men like Dan in mind—men who liked pictures of gorgeous women. And, more specifically, men who wanted to convince their own gorgeous significant other that golf could be fun for women. Or at least that golf instructors were really good looking.

"How long have you been plotting this?" Beth said, tossing the brochure back without looking inside. "When did you get that brochure?"

Dan ignored her questions. "You're between jobs right now, so I thought it would be a good time," he said instead. "And I have too much vacation time built up. I need to take some time off or I'll lose it. I think we should go to Palm Springs this fall and take couple's lessons."

"Or we could go to the Westminster Dog Show. Maybe you'll see a dog breed you like," Beth countered.

"It's not about breeds. It's about the species." He pointed at ChiChi. "They're messy. Golf? You put the clubs in the garage, change your shoes, and you get on with your day. Dogs—it's not so easy. Whenever you go somewhere, you have to put the dog in a kennel. We can't even go out to dinner without having to hurry home to let ChiChi out. Not to mention the ridiculous dog hair everywhere."

ChiChi lifted her head briefly at the mention of her name, but quickly let it drop again with a thud against the deck boards.

"That's why I shouldn't take up golf," Beth argued. "It's a day-long commitment. ChiChi would be cooped up inside all day. And I already have no time to see my friends. Not to mention that golf is expensive."

At that, Dan smirked. "Do you recall how much you spent on ChiChi's last vet visit? And she's not even your dog!"

"Touché." Beth hated it when Dan used that tone of voice—the one that sounded like he was all reason and logic and smarts, and she needed a scolding like a child. She picked up the brochure again. "But how much is this golf school?"

"Less than ChiChi's root canal."

"Not funny," Beth muttered. She opened the brochure and started to read. What Dan said made some sense. They did need to find new ways to engage with each other now that the initial spark of their romance had cooled—as unimpressive as it was in the first place. Maybe she could learn to play golf. Maybe she could get good at it. She used to play tennis, and she used to think she was fairly athletic.

But even if she did take up the game, she had no plans to give up on dogs. If she could play golf, he could put up with ChiChi.

Two

THE STARBUCKS EMPLOYEE CAFETERIA WAS in a big industrial space with huge ducts painted in bright primary colors overhead and concrete floors underfoot. Beth tried to smile at everyone who looked her way. She had no idea who might be interviewing her that afternoon, and which of these people she'd be working with soon, if she were lucky enough to get the job.

Ever since she'd stepped inside the building an hour before, she'd been envious—not so much of the subsidized lunch or the open floorplan, but of the company badges everyone else wore. The paper visitor tag stuck to the lapel of her jacket made her stick out as an outsider.

It had been a few months since she'd worn a corporate badge at her former company. Once she'd been furloughed in the pandemic, the company decided she wasn't needed—permanently. With all corporate meetings cancelled, no one needed an events coordinator, and once companies learned that their business could continue fine by Zoom, she got the bad news in writing.

"This is no reflection on your performance, and it does not affect the amount of severance you will be paid per your employment contract," the bad-news letter concluded. Her former boss called and assured her that she would receive an enthusiastic review if anyone called for a reference. Now, the severance money was quickly running out, and it had taken longer than she had hoped for employers to get back to scheduling employee marketing or customer events. A chance at this dream job—at a successful company with a worldwide brand in what was reportedly a fun working environment—was almost too good to be true.

"Are you nervous?" her friend Debra asked, as they finished the French fries they were sharing for lunch along with their healthy but uninspiring salads.

"Oddly not," Beth said. "Should I be? I mean, I really want this job, but I've been doing this sort of thing for five years. Surely I'm qualified."

"You wouldn't have gotten the interview if you weren't. Just remember, a lot of the interview will be about whether you're a 'good fit'—not about your experience of qualifications."

"Well, how do I prove I'm a good fit? How will I know what it looks like?"

"You won't. But the interviewer has a list of things to look for."

"Do you know what they are?"

Debra laughed. "Heck no! Every department is different, and every manager has his own quirks. You're about to learn the meaning of serendipity, my friend. Either you fit or you don't."

"Seems more like luck of the draw than serendipity," Beth mused.

"Well, just be yourself. If you're not a good fit, you don't

want the job anyway. It wouldn't be any fun. Most important is to convince them you're a team player. Team is everything around here."

Beth sank into her own thoughts. She wasn't necessarily a social butterfly and, in fact, was at times socially awkward, which made her choice of a career in event planning a
bit ironic. But she'd always gotten along with her co-workers at big events by grinning and bearing—and going home
afterwards to a cold bottle of sauvignon blanc.

"I'm glad I got this interview today," Beth said, shifting
topics. "We're leaving tomorrow."

"The golf trip?" Deb flashed a sympathetic smile.
"You're really going through with this?"

"If nothing else, it will be nice to be in the sun for a
week. If I flunk out of the golf lessons, I'll sit by the pool
and drink cocktails with little umbrellas."

Deb sighed, jealous. "Maybe I should come with you.
I could use some warm-weather R&R. But I'm not crazy
about this golf thing. I'm afraid you'll really like it and we'll
never have time together anymore. You'll be on the golf
course with Dan all the time."

"If I get this job, then we'll see each other at lunch every day. And I doubt I'll be good enough after a week that
Dan will want to play with me."

"I don't know," Debra said. "You've always struck me
as pretty athletic. I'll bet you're a natural. Is Ellen taking
ChiChi for you?"

"Yes, Mom loves her."

Beth glanced at her watch. "Whoops, you'd better run.
I'll get your tray. Run upstairs now or you'll be late for your
interview."

THE NEXT MORNING WAS RAINY again, and Beth had to run
in the dark from Dan's car to her mom's front door, hoping
ChiChi's thick coat wouldn't soak up too much water. She

had the dog's rain coat in the bag she'd prepared for Chi-Chi's visit, but she didn't have time to put it on her before Dan rushed them out of her apartment.

The door was unlocked, and Beth let herself in. ChiChi ran past her mom and headed for the spot in the kitchen where her food bowl was kept.

"So that's my hello?" Ellen said, looking at the dog's wet trail.

"Hi, Mom." Beth leaned in and kissed her mother on the cheek. "Here's the leash, some pills for anxiety, and some treats."

"Anxiety?" They followed ChiChi to the kitchen.

"Yeah, I actually think it only happens around Dan, but you never know."

"I'll have to admit, I'm surprised Dan is letting you travel with him," her mom said, putting the big bag of dog stuff on the kitchen counter.

"Well, we're getting separate rooms," Beth said, "so he didn't have to explain something embarrassing to his mom."

"That doesn't surprise me," Ellen said, shaking her head. "How did my little bohemian end up with Dan?"

Beth just shrugged.

"You're coming back when?"

"Saturday. A week from tomorrow. Dan wants to get back in time to have a day in the office by himself before the week starts."

"You mean on Sunday?"

"Yup. Oh, and by the way, he still doesn't know that I've adopted ChiChi. He thinks I'm still just fostering her. So don't say anything to him."

"Doesn't he wonder why no one has taken her yet? She's so gorgeous!" Ellen bent down, her face close to Chi-Chi's. "You know you're gorgeous, don't you?" She rubbed noses with the dog.

"Dan's so blind to dogs, he can't see how wonderful she

is," Beth said. "Especially for a malamute. They can be so difficult."

"I never thought I'd see you with someone who doesn't like dogs," Ellen said, straightening up.

"Okay, Mom. Enough Dan-criticism already. I've got to run. We're catching that seven a.m. flight to Palm Springs." She bent down and hugged ChiChi.

"You be a good girl for Grandma, okay Sweetie," she said. ChiChi followed her to the door. "Bye, Mom."

Beth leaned in to kiss her mother on the cheek again and ran outside through the downpour to the car. She jumped in and brushed water off her coat.

"You're getting the seat all wet," Dan said, putting the car in gear.

Beth looked at him, puzzled. "Sorry. What do you want me to do? Levitate?"

Dan grimaced with disgust and shook his head. He pulled away from the curb. The rain pelted the windshield, and Beth watched it wash in sheets off the streets and sidewalks into the gutters.

"I don't know if I'll ever take to golf, but I'll sure be glad to get out of this rain for a week," she said, glumly.

"I predict you're going to like golf. A few lessons can make all the difference," Dan said. "I might have trouble getting you to come back here."

"If it were all about the weather, I think you're right. I've lived here all my life, and sometimes even I get sick of the rain."

Dan leaned forward to look up through the splattered windshield at the dark sky. "Sorry I had to work so late last night," he said. "I needed to get the team all set before we left."

"That's okay. I went to bed early. I was really tired."

"How'd the interview go yesterday?"

"I don't really know. I think I had answers for all their

questions. But Debra said something about how it all comes down to 'the right fit.'"

Dan nodded. "Yes, it does." He probably knew, Beth thought. He'd been part of that kind of corporate world for more than a decade at Amazon's headquarters.

"How do you figure out if someone's the 'right fit?'" she asked.

"If it's a guy, I like to play golf with him. You can learn a lot about a person on the golf course that you can't learn in an interview." He stopped briefly at a red light and turned right onto the highway toward the airport.

"And if it's a woman? You don't take her on the golf course?"

"Most of the women I interview don't play golf."

"Then you do you determine 'fit' if she doesn't?"

As usual, Dan ignored the question he didn't want to answer. "See that's another reason why you should learn to play golf. It will give you a leg up on the competition when you're looking for a job."

"Well, only if the guy who's hiring is a man who plays golf," she said, trying to keep the sarcasm out of her voice. It was early. They had eight days together in front of them. Striving for a more neutral tone, she added, "I doubt that one week of lessons is going to make much of a difference."

"If you go in with that attitude, it probably won't," he said, reaching across the console to grab her hand. "Come on. Promise me you'll try."

Three

BETH AND DAN DUCKED THROUGH the downpour into the departure terminal in Seattle and shook themselves off in a way that reminded her of ChiChi. Three hours later, their coats tucked into garbage bags and stuffed into outside pockets of their suitcases, they walked out of the Palm Springs Airport terminal into bright sunshine.

"Now, this is more like it!" Beth exclaimed. She pulled her phone out of her purse and turned it on. "It's 85 degrees here! I haven't seen 85 since that one day in August."

She stuck her phone into the back pocket of her jeans and looked up at the bright blue sky, the steep grey-brown slope of mountains just west of the town, and the palm trees swaying in the breeze.

"I could get used to this," she said.

Dan was paying no attention to her, focused as he was on reading emails on his phone. He looked up just as a town car pulled up to the curb with his name taped to the window, and a driver in uniform hopped out.

"You ordered a town car?" Beth asked. "What are we? Celebrities?"

"It's a perk of being a big wig at Amazon," Dan said, rather smugly. "Don't complain. It's much more comfortable than a cab."

"What's wrong with Uber?"

Dan stepped off the curb and shook the driver's hand. As Beth slid into the back seat, Dan stood watching the man load their golf clubs and suitcases into the trunk. He got in beside her when the trunk slammed closed.

"So, is this how it goes when you travel for work?" she asked.

"Pretty much. Why? Does it bother you?"

Beth shrugged and looked away, out the window as the driver pulled out and turned the air conditioning up to gale force.

"You'll get used to it," Dan said before turning back to his cell phone.

Beth watched as they rolled past vast, empty desertscapes next to huge residential developments, some that looked sad and aging and some brand new—so new that the tops of the replanted palm trees were still tied into tight, upright ponytails.

Twenty minutes later, they pulled up to the Westin Hotel, its shady, arched portico leading back past the check-in lobby and the time-share sales office toward the restaurants and swimming pools.

"We're staying here?" Beth asked. Suddenly she felt like a rube. How could anyone spend their entire life in a sophisticated city like Seattle and never stay a single night in a fancy resort hotel? she wondered. She'd organized plenty of events at them, but she'd never once been a guest at one. Perhaps getting married to Dan would come with benefits she'd never imagined.

The driver opened her door first, and she stepped out to look down a cascading fountain at a wide, lush lawn between rows of majestic palms. The whole watery display seemed to serve no purpose other than decoration.

"I thought this was a desert," she mused, only realizing she'd said it out loud when Dan grabbed her arm.

"Yup, it is," he said brusquely. "Let's hurry. I'm starving. We have just enough time for lunch before we meet the instructor on the driving range this afternoon."

"Don't we have to check in?"

"All taken care of," Dan said.

As they walked down the arched portico to the restaurant, Beth wondered why Dan always seemed so tired when he got home from his business trips. This kind of travel seemed awfully easy to her.

Beth watched with embarrassment as Dan shoveled his lunch soup and sandwich down as if a wildfire was approaching and it would be his last meal for the foreseeable future. For all his advanced degrees and all of his sophistication when it came to business, he easily slipped into a kind of bachelor, barbarian comportment when no one but she was looking.

"You have soup on your shirt." She pointed to the orange tomato stain just below the buttons of his golf polo.

Dan dabbed at it ineffectively with his napkin and pointed at her salad.

"Better hurry," he said. "I don't want to be late. Jake is very popular and we're lucky to get him."

"Jake?"

"Our golf instructor. Didn't you read the confirmation letter?"

"Yes, but I guess I didn't memorize it."

Dan slurped the last of his soup and tossed down his spoon. "I sure hope you get your heart into this, or it will turn out to be a big waste of money," he said, wiping his chin.

"It wasn't my idea to spend this kind of money on golf lessons," she reminded him.

Dan grabbed the leather portfolio the waiter had left with their lunch check, threw in some tens, and snapped it closed. "Come on now. Eat up. We should get going."

"I'm finished," Beth said, folding up her napkin and laying it across her plate. "Not impressed with this salad anyway."

Four

Following Dan down the slope from the restaurant to the roped-off lesson area, Beth glanced over at the pool complex. It looked heavenly.

It was noon, and most of the lounge chairs were still unoccupied. Only a handful of people sat at the bar tables under colorful umbrellas. She heard a whir of a margarita machine and the clink of ice cubes being scooped into glass. Perhaps she would be over there soon. If she could just get through this first afternoon and show Dan that he'd be happier taking lessons without her.

The man Beth assumed was Jake stood before a large pile of golf balls, swinging an iron back and forth with an ease that made it look like he'd been born with a club in his hand. He turned as they approached, and Dan strutted forward, his hand extended. He grabbed Jake's and pumped.

"Hi, I'm Dan Norris," he nearly shouted. "And this is my fiancé." Either his adrenaline was spiking at the thought of showing off his golf swing or that tomato soup was full of amphetamines.

Beth walked up behind him and shook Jake's hand, considerably less excitedly. "I'm Beth. I think Dan forgets I have a name sometimes."

Jake winked at her. "You might be surprised how common that is," he said. He stood back, his club still in his hand and looked them over.

"Welcome, Dan and Beth," he said. "I see you're from Seattle. I'll bet this sunshine feels pretty good."

Beth smiled and nodded. She liked the look of the instructor, even if she wasn't terribly excited about why they'd been brought together. Just a few wisps of dark hair curled out from under his golf cap, framing a nicely tanned, lean face. His strong cheekbones framed a wide smile and left just enough room for his Ray-bans to rest on his nose like an eyeglass model. He was tall with a muscular chest and long, sinewy arms. He continued to flick the club a few inches back and forth. Was it nervous energy, or had he swung a club so many times in his professional career that he didn't even realize when he was doing it?

"As you probably read in the brochure, I am Jake Engels, and I am going to help you take whatever golf game you came with to a new level this week," he said. "We'll work hard, but we'll have some fun too."

Beth hadn't come in feeling very positive about that, but Jake's gorgeous smile was changing things. On the other hand, Dan's feet were shifting impatiently. He kept looking at his clubs as if he couldn't wait to start pounding balls out onto the driving range.

"I think you should know," she answered. "I really don't have a golf game. I'm pretty much starting from zero. Or less than zero."

Jake's grin seemed to get even bigger. How was that possible?

"Not a problem!" he said. "I've helped people who didn't even know what end of the club to hold. Most get to the point that they enjoy the game. The good thing is that golf is one of those things you don't have to be really good at to enjoy."

"Can we cut the chit-chat and get started?" Dan interrupted. "I'm paying for instruction, not for cheerleading."

Jake took the jab well. "Sure, Dan. I understand," he said, his voice unchanged. "Why don't the two of you grab your favorite club from your bag and warm up a bit. I'd like to watch your swings so I have a bit of an idea of where we're starting from."

Beth watched Dan pull his driver out of his bag and step a few feet away to take some warm-up swings. She didn't have a "favorite club," so she followed his lead and grabbed her driver too.

Jake came up beside her and reached into her bag, pulling out an iron.

"Why don't you take the seven iron," he said, handing it to her. "It's a nice, comfortable club to hit. A mid-iron. Probably an easier place to start."

Beth nodded and stepped up to a pyramid of balls on the tee. She watched Dan put a tee in the ground on the next tee over, knock some balls off his pyramid, and put one on a tee. He took another practice swing, lined up for a shot and swung. Beth had been intimidated by his golf prowess before, and now she didn't feel any better. She doubted she'd ever be able to swing that fast or hit the ball that hard. The ball flew out to the right side of the driving range and landed somewhere beyond where Beth could see.

She looked over at Jake and shrugged. He smiled and nodded at her pyramid of balls. "Go ahead. Just swing easy," he said. Could he read her mind already?

Beth reached down and took the top ball off the pyramid and put it on the grass. She was happy she knew enough about golf to not use a tee with an iron. She stood back for a practice swing and tried to swing the club fast and hard like Dan did. She felt silly, but she stepped up to the ball and swung again. The club hit the ball and skidded forward about 25 yards, never leaving the ground.

She turned to Jake and raised her arms. "See! I'm no good. I shouldn't even be out here."

Dan lined up to take another shot with his driver, and Beth turned to watch.

"Beth, isn't it?" Jake said.

"Yes."

"Beth, don't watch Dan. You aren't going to learn anything that way. Just go ahead and hit a few more balls. Slow and easy. And don't be so nervous. No one is watching but me, and I've seen people whiff the ball a dozen times in a row. You made contact, and that's a good sign."

Beth did as she was told and was relieved to see Jake move over behind Dan to watch him instead. She took a deep breath and lined up another shot.

"Nice swing, Dan," Jake said. "I think if you slowed it down just a tad and stayed in the shot just a split second longer, you'll get a little more accuracy and less of a slice."

Dan twirled around and lifted his chin. "It's not a slice. It's a fade," he said. "I do that on purpose."

"Great," Jake said, rewarding Dan's confidence with a big smile. "If you're going for the power fade, perhaps aim a little more to the left then, and you'll end up closer to the middle."

"Are you serious?" Dan sounded angry. "Let me ask you something, Jake. What's your handicap?"

Beth listened closely. She knew Dan bragged about his "single-digit" handicap, which was a nine—just barely single-digit. He'd told her it meant he generally could expect to score nine strokes over par in an 18-hole round.

"I'm a plus two," Jake said, nonchalantly. Beth knew

what that meant, too: Jake would generally expect to finish a round a couple of strokes under par. That, she knew, was the kind of handicap professional golfers had, but one that was rare for amateurs like Dan. "What's yours?"

"Uh …" Dan muttered something that Beth couldn't hear and lined up his next shot a little to the left, and his slice—or was it a fade?—sent the ball right down the middle.

"Well, look at that," Jake teased. "Just like you planned it."

Dan pretended not to hear him and knocked another ball off the pyramid. Jake moved back over behind Beth.

"How's it going here, Beth?" he asked.

"I don't think I'm learning anything," she said, shrugging again.

"Yeah, I just wanted you to warm up a bit. Now, let me show you the first thing I want you to learn." Jake moved in behind her, his long arms along her sides. He shook her club loose from her hand, and stood it upright, holding it with just an index finger in front of her.

"Put your left hand on the grip like this," he said. He demonstrated and then moved his hand away.

Beth felt his warm torso against her back and wondered how she was supposed to concentrate on the club, but she tried to follow. "Like this?" she asked.

"Yes, but looser. Don't squeeze," he said. "Now put your right hand over the left thumb like this." As she tried to imitate his placement, he gently lifted her right thumb and moved it counterclockwise.

Jake backed away, and Beth felt the air cool against her back. Was she sweating?

"There," he said. "Now waggle the club a little and see how that feels."

Beth lifted the club off the ground and swayed it back and forth. "Weird," she said. "It feels weird."

"That's because you've gotten used to a bad grip," Jake explained. "The grip is what sets up the entire golf swing. Without a good grip, we put ourselves at a disadvantage from the start."

Beth looked up as she waggled the club and saw Dan watching her, frowning.

"Don't stand with your feet so far apart." He pointed at his own feet. "More like this."

"Dan," she said. She dismissed him with a wave. "I'm listening to Jake here."

"I know," Dan insisted. "But your stance isn't any good."

"Dan is right," Jake said, stepping in between them to block Dan's view. "But let's take one step at a time here. Now, with your new grip, take a full swing, just to get a feel for it."

Beth started to swing, and Jake walked back behind Dan. "Dan, I see you're driving the ball well. How's your short game? Chipping? Putting?"

"Not as good," Dan admitted.

"Why don't you grab a short iron and show me your approach shot," he said, pointing at Dan's bag. "Maybe hit a few hundred-yard shots. Take a few practice shots, and I'll be right back with you."

"Now, Beth," he said, moving back to face her. "Let me see how that grip is holding up."

A couple of hours later, Beth had started to get more comfortable with the new grip, and Jake had given her a few more tips about turning her shoulders and keeping her left arm straight. She was starting to get tired, though, and she paused longer and longer between shots. Finally, she let her club fall down and shook her arms.

"My hands are getting sore," she said. "Do you think maybe we've done enough?"

"You're gripping the club too tight," Dan shouted over his shoulder. "Loosen up a little."

Beth watched as Jake shook his head, took a deep breath, and winked at her.

"I think that's all for this afternoon, anyway," he said. "Let's call it a day." He bent down and picked up the clubs Beth had left lying by her golf bag. He stuck them back where they belonged and handed her a towel.

"So. I'll see you folks bright and early tomorrow," he said. "Eight-thirty. Is that okay?"

"I'm not sure this is a good idea, guys," she said, looking at Dan. "Why don't you just take the lessons. I'll come and watch some, but I don't think I'm going to like this."

"Absolutely not," Jake interjected before Dan could answer. "You've already made a ton of progress, Beth. I won't take no for an answer. I'll see you both tomorrow morning. Have a great evening, you two."

He turned and started to walk back toward the clubhouse but, after a few steps, he stopped and looked back at them. "Just leave your bags here," he said. "I'll have the bag guys come and get them for you. We'll store them overnight."

"Thanks," Beth called after him.

Dan put his arm over Beth's shoulders and steered her up the slope. "He's right, Beth. Don't get discouraged. It takes a lot of practice, but you can get there. Come on. Let's go get a cocktail at the hotel."

Maybe, Beth thought. Maybe she could "get there" if Dan would get off her ass. She'd give it one more day—or at least one morning. And then, if it still seemed hopeless, she'd head for the pools and that drink she'd been dreaming of. The one with the umbrella.

Five

MIDWAY THROUGH THE LESSON THE next morning, even
Beth could tell she was improving. Dan was slamming ball
after ball down the practice range, signaling clearly that
he didn't think Jake could teach him anything. But as Jake
stood next to Beth to show her how to move her hips as she
swung, Dan stepped toward them.

"You need to pause a little bit at the top, Beth," Dan
said.

He took his own club back and held it at the top of his
backswing to show her. It was the third time he had butted
in that morning, and it wasn't helping Beth concentrate on
Jake's advice.

But it was Jake who protested.

"Dan, we're going to make no progress here if you keep
throwing in your two cents." He waved Dan back.

"Well, when I see she's doing something wrong—" Dan
started to explain.

"And how has that worked in the past?" Jake asked. "Has she had trouble learning from you before?"

Beth was surprised when Dan stepped back, chagrined. "I just want to help," he said weakly.

"I know you do. But this isn't helping. I'm happy to work with both of you, but I have to ask you to back off when I'm working with Beth."

Dan looked away and sighed. It didn't seem like he was having any fun.

"How about if I just go up and see if I can get a tee-time?" he said. "I'm kind of tired of practicing."

"Sounds like a good idea, Dan," Jake said. "I think the main purpose here is for Beth to learn. Am I right?"

Dan and Beth both nodded.

"So, why don't you go play, and we'll continue here? I'm happy to give you a refund for half the price of these lessons."

"No, that's okay," Dan said, dropping his clubs back into his bag. "A one-on-one lesson costs about the same as for two. I'm glad to pay. You just help Beth."

"Great," Jake said as Dan pulled the bag over his shoulder and headed up the hill. "Thanks, Dan."

Beth and Jake watched him retreat toward the clubhouse, and Beth let out a sign of relief.

"Have fun, honey," she called after him. "I'll see you at cocktail hour."

Once Dan was safely out of earshot, she turned to Jake. "Thanks. You don't know how hard—"

"No problem." Jake cut her off. "You'll never know how common that is. You can't learn from your spouse—male or female. It's not possible. Now, let's get back to work. You're making incredible progress already."

Jake took the club she was holding out of her hand and handed her a different one from her bag. "You're really quite athletic," he said. "What other sports do you play?"

"None," she answered. "I ride a bike, hike. But I used to play a little tennis. Back when I was in college."

"Ah. That makes sense. That hand-eye coordination is important in golf, too. Why don't we work another hour, have lunch, and then go out on the course this afternoon?"

"Do you think I'm ready? I still can't hit the ball very far."

"No, you can't," Jake said. "But I want you to enjoy the game, not just hit balls. We can just do a few holes, if you'd like. And we can play a scramble."

"What's that?"

"You hit, I hit, and then we take our next shot from the spot of the best one." He pointed to the club in her hand. "Now, let's work a little more on your follow-through."

Beth was happy the morning's lesson was over. Once again, her arms and hands were tired, and hitting the ball out into the big grass range was starting to feel monotonous. As she sat with Jake on the patio and sipped a grapefruit juice and vodka, she relaxed, knowing they weren't going to return to the range that afternoon.

"What made you decide to take golf lessons?" Jake asked after the waiter had taken their order for sandwiches.

"Well, we're supposed to be getting married ..." She let her voice trail. Suddenly she wasn't sure this was something she wanted Jake to know. Why not? she wondered. Was she—could she be—so quickly attracted to him? He was a golf instructor. He was supposed to be congenial and a bit of a flirt. Caught in thought, she didn't finish her sentence.

"Congratulations," Jake said. "Supposed to?"

"'Supposed to,' yes," she said. "I'm not as sure as Dan, but that's neither here nor there." She tried to adopt a breezy, devil-may-care tone. "Dan thought we needed to have more things in common. So, golf it is."

"It is a great sport for couples," Jake agreed.

"I suppose. So, do you play with your wife? Partner? A girlfriend? Anyone play golf with you?"

He grinned. Had she been too transparent?

"No, I just came off the tour. Haven't had any time to meet anyone. And trust me, you don't want to date any of those women who follow the tour around. They're looking for one thing."

"What?"

"Money."

Beth chuckled at herself. She had expected him to say "sex." Why was that? How silly could she be?

"Of course," Jake continued, "they would have figured out pretty quickly that I wasn't making much."

Beth laughed. He was certainly modest. It only added to his appeal. Too bad that hadn't rubbed off on Dan a little.

"So, you played on the PGA Tour?"

Jake shook his head. "Not the regular tour. I never got past the Korn Ferry Tour." He looked up at her blank expression. "It's like the minors in baseball."

"Wow, you hit the ball as well as you do, and you got stuck in the minors?"

"Well, it takes a lot more than hitting the ball to succeed."

Beth nodded. She'd heard this before. "You mean 90 percent mental, like Dan always says?"

"Yup, that's exactly what I mean," Jake said as the waiter put their sandwiches down. "Now, let's eat and then we'll go see what we can do out there on the course."

Six

THE THREE HOURS BETH SPENT playing with Jake that afternoon were like none she'd ever spent on a golf course before.

They were fun.

As she stood up to the first tee box, her hands shook so violently that she was afraid she would drop the club. Jake stood in front of her and put his hand on hers, stopping her before she swung at the ball.

"Let's go for less than driver," he said.

She looked up, puzzled. "What do you mean?"

He took the driver out of her hands and replaced it with a five-wood out of her bag. "Drivers are hard to hit. I know men who never use them, and many women prefer the smaller head of a fairway wood."

Beth had to admit: it felt intimidating to swing the huge head of her driver at the ball. Not only did it seem too big for the task, the shaft was the longest of any of her clubs. With that much distance between her arms and the ball, it seemed unlikely she'd hit anything.

"Take a practice swing with that one and let your arms relax," Jake said.

Beth shook her arms to release the tension, but her heart was still racing. "I feel naked," she muttered.

"Everyone does," Jake answered. "It's called Naked on the First Tee. There's a book by that title. Let your shoulders drop. That will help."

Standing over the ball, she looked up at him and grimaced. "There are too many things to think about!"

"Don't think," he said. "Just relax and watch the clubhead hit the ball."

"What if I miss?"

"Then you can try again."

Beth took a deep breath, let her shoulders drop from her ears where they'd been stuck, and swung. Miraculously, the ball sailed forward and straight. She stood watching it fly and then roll down the fairway. She'd never hit a shot like that when she'd played with Dan. Ever.

"Wow," Jake said, his hands on his hips, watching with her. "See what you can do? Let's go play that ball!"

"But aren't you going to drive?" she asked. "You can hit it much farther."

"Sure, I can, but I think we should take advantage of that great drive. Come on, jump in." He hopped behind the steering wheel, and she barely got in before he gunned the cart.

Most of her shots that afternoon were much less glorious than that first one off the tee. But instead of turning grouchy, as Dan always did when she whiffed the ball or hit it sideways, Jake just laughed, and she laughed with him.

At first, when she lined up for her shots, his eyes on her made her nervous. But after he praised her few good ones, she looked forward to performing for him. If she hit a horrid shot, he threw down another ball for her to hit and told her to relax. Indeed, relaxing was the key to playing well, she discovered as they went along. "It's a stupid game" was Jake's mantra, which took the seriousness out of the silly venture. The more she laughed, smiled, and relaxed, the better she played.

Halfway down the last fairway, Beth was tired. It was only a par-three, and after her tee shot, her ball still sat sixty yards from the green. A good shot with her wedge should have put the ball near the pin, but instead, she shanked it into the bushes on the right.

"I'm spent!" she said, letting her club fall to the ground.

"Yes, I can see that," Jake said. He walked up to her and picked up the club. "Here, let me show you something." He handed her the club and stood behind her, putting his hands over hers on the club. He started a backswing as if they were going to hit together and stopped when Beth thought the club was only halfway back.

"See this?" he said, holding the club still. "This is as far as you need to take the club back. In fact, when you're tired, you try too hard and you swing too big. Remember, less is sometimes more."

Slightly dizzy, Beth turned her head to face him. His arms stayed along her sides, their faces only inches apart. For a long moment, they held their position, searching the other's eyes.

Beth fought the urge to lean forward just a little and brush her lips against his. And yet, at the same time, she feared he was going to kiss her. But she couldn't move.

Jake smiled, relieving the tension, let go of her club, and backed away.

"I'm sorry," Jake said, looking away. "I didn't mean to do that." His shyness was part of his charm. Unlike Dan, he didn't show any evidence of what her fiancé had displayed as a sense of entitlement to any space he wanted to occupy.

"That's too bad," she half-teased. "I was hoping you did."

"Let's go putt," he said, waving at the green and avoiding her eyes. "The only way to end a round is with the sound of that ball going in the hole."

As they drove the long nine-hole distance back to the clubhouse, she put a hand on his forearm. "Thanks, Jake. I had so much more fun than I expected."

"I'm glad you enjoyed it," he said. It seemed he had regained his composure. "See, the secret is taking the pressure off yourself. Just enjoy the swing. How many times in your day do you get to do something so free and physical as swinging a golf club?"

"I am starting to get that feeling. Is that what Dan feels? Is that why he likes it so much?"

"I don't know Dan very well, but at his level, he probably really enjoys competing. Remember how he asked me what my handicap was?"

"Yeah, why?"

"Well, a guy does that if he's trying to prove something to himself. It's a way of competing without even swinging a club. You just compare numbers. He probably does that on the course, too. And that's okay. It's a game. You can play it to compete, or you can just play it to enjoy swinging the club or to take in the beauty of the golf course."

Beth looked out at the green fairways as they zipped down the cart path, past holes 10 through 18.

"It is a lot more peaceful out here than I ever knew," she said quietly. "It helps if you don't have someone yelling at you every time you take a swing."

"I'm sorry that's what has happened," Jake said. "But you and Dan seem happy together otherwise. Maybe this will bring you closer together."

"That's what Dan thinks. That's why we're here. To get closer together. We're supposed to get married."

"'Supposed to' again?"

Watching Jake squint as he took that in, she wondered if she should talk about her ambivalence over her marriage. Jake was not only kind and patient, but got better looking and nicer the closer she got to him.

"It's good to share hobbies," he said, ignoring her stare. "What else do you two share?"

"Not much. We're both pretty serious about our careers. I love books, but Dan doesn't read. I love dogs, and Dan really doesn't like them. He loves golf, but up until today, I didn't have much to say for it."

"Well, there! We've made progress already!"

Jake laughed and Beth had a close up look at the smile that intrigued her the afternoon before. How long had they known each other? It had been just over twenty-four hours, she realized, and yet here she was, more comfortable sitting in the cart next to him than she ever was sitting in one next to Dan.

"It is a great sport whatever your skill," he said.

"I suppose," she said. "But is teaching beginners like me any fun?"

Jake looked at her and smiled as he pulled up to the cart barn. "With beginners like you who learn so fast, yes, it's fun."

"I can see why you teach, Jake. You are really good at this."

They had just enough time to exchange affectionate grins before Dan ran up to their cart and opened his arms to Beth, begging a hug.

"You won't believe how great I played today!" he exclaimed.

She wondered how long it would be before he thought to ask how her game had gone.

Seven

DAN WAS IN HIGH SPIRITS after his afternoon golf game, surprising Beth. She was used to him complaining about how he played, which never seemed to be as well as he thought he should.

As they settled at a table in the middle of a white-tablecloth restaurant in a high-end hotel in Palm Desert, he reached over the table with one hand and wove his fingers into hers.

"You look gorgeous tonight," he said, his eyes soft.

Beth grimaced. That schmaltzy look was usually a precursor to another insistence that they talk about a wedding date. She decided to preempt it by encouraging a recap of how he had scored on all eighteen holes that afternoon. His play-by-play usually bored her to tears.

"Did you have fun today?" she asked.

"Yeah. I got paired up with a couple of guys. Great golfers. I think we're going to go out again tomorrow morning."

"Who won?"

"Won? You've never asked me that before," he smiled brightly, looking both surprised and pleased.

'Well, I think I'm starting to understand what attracts you to the game. You like the competition.'

At that, he chuckled condescendingly. Beth decided to let it pass. She was in a good mood, and her afternoon on the course was the reason, too.

"Of course. It's a game. That's what games are. Competitions."

The waiter delivered a glass of wine for Beth and a beer for Dan, and they studied their menus. Beth settled quickly on the sand dabs, an expensive entré that Dan was unlikely to oppose, given the good mood he was in.

Why am I attracted to him? she wondered as she watched him look over the menu items and sip his beer. She tried to remember back to three years before, when she first saw him at a company picnic she was catering at Amazon. He worked there with Jason, Deb's boyfriend, and Deb was anxious to introduce them.

"He's going places in that company," Deb had assured her. "I guess he's really good at what he does, and you know he's got to have a fortune in stock options."

Beth had argued that, in her experience, rich men weren't easy to like and were usually too full of themselves to leave room for anyone else's personality.

"That's not fair." Deb repeated the old mantra: "It's as easy to fall in love with a rich man as a poor one."

Despite her expectation that she would be disappointed, she found Dan surprisingly accommodating that afternoon. He wasn't dismissive of her work in catering, which she expected him to be, and he hung around the food table. On a date a week later, he asked about her family and her past, something that men often didn't do until they had finally finished delivering a full narrative of their own lives.

When they took a kayak out on the lake a sunny Labor Day another week later, Dan took his shirt off to soak up the sun. Sitting behind him, she was surprised by the muscles in his back and arms and chastised herself for her assumption that guys like him—corporate executives—couldn't be fit. Where did that come from? Even though Dan had risen in the company to where he was heading up operations of one of the company's retail divisions, it was clear that he not only saw the inside of a gym, but that he spent a considerable amount of time there.

After that, they started seeing each other every week, usually for dinner, and gradually, their relationship progressed to nearly daily meetings, only interrupted by Dan's frequent business trips, and evenings when Beth had to supervise company events. She welcomed their growing commitment at first, but once Dan started badgering her about getting married, she felt herself pulling back. Was this commitment phobia? Or was she just growing bored with him? He was smart, rich, and ambitious; but he was also uninterested in the wine, books, and dogs—her three passions. He had no travel bug and had actually told her once he had no desire to go anywhere he'd hadn't been before.

But perhaps predictably, the more she pulled away, the closer he clung. And slowly she figured out something: he wanted to be sure his future at Amazon wasn't jeopardized by an impression that he didn't have a stable family life. Ironic, Beth thought. As if Jeff Bezos was some kind of role model.

She figured that someday she would get married. And eventually she might even decide to have children—or a child. But first, she wanted to travel and get her own career on track.

But the biggest obstacle to their union was Dan's dislike—or at least indifference to—ChiChi. How could she ever commit to living the rest of her life without a canine best friend? She hadn't lived without one in the house her entire life. Dan was the only reason she had decided to foster ChiChi at first, instead of adopting her after her last dog died.

Dan put down his menu and leaned forward, his smile still reflecting his great day on the golf course.

"I think you'd really like George," he said.

"Who's George?"

"One of the guys I played with today. He's smart and funny. He used to work in L.A. for a software company."

"So, you had a lot in common, I guess?"

"Yeah, project management headaches. And golf." Dan tipped up his glass and drained his beer. "We're at about the same level. Same handicap."

"Oh." That handicap comparison thing again. If men weren't measuring themselves against each other in some such way, how would they know who was on top?

Dan signaled for the waiter, and they ordered dinner. Dan asked for another beer.

"And you, miss?" the waiter asked.

"Nah, I'm driving," she said. It wasn't true—they were taking cabs. But Dan didn't correct her. She twirled what was left of the wine in her glass and took a sip.

The waiter left. "Oh, hey," Dan said. "I forgot to ask. How'd the rest of our lesson go this afternoon?"

Beth used her napkin to wipe the smile off her face. She didn't want to raise any suspicions about how much she had enjoyed Jake's undivided attention. She lowered her voice.

"Great. We went out on the course this afternoon. Just nine holes."

"Wow. Were you ready for that?"

"What do you mean?"

"Well, you weren't hitting the ball that well yesterday."

Beth pushed his insult aside. "Didn't matter," she said. "Do you know what a scramble is?"

"Of course. I've been playing golf since I was five."

"Well, anyway, that took all the pressure off. And I hit some pretty good shots."

"Of course, Jake must have made it easy," Dan said. "You probably played from all his shots."

"Nope," she said. "If I hit a good one, we used it. Sometimes he didn't even hit."

"That's wonderful."

"We're going to do the same thing tomorrow. Driving range in the morning and another nine holes in the afternoon."

"Okay. So, you don't want me to come back to the lesson?" If Dan was jealous of how much she was enjoying playing with Jake, it didn't show.

"Do you want to?" she asked.

"Not really. I don't think Jake had much to teach me," he said to Beth's relief. "I'd rather join George and Ryan again. If that's okay with you. You don't think I'm abandoning you, do you?"

"No, it's fine," she said, trying again to hide a smile. "You and I are at two totally different levels, anyway, and—"

"Oh, I almost forgot," he interrupted. "We're going to join the guys for dinner Monday night. They know this great hamburger spot in La Quinta, and they want to meet you."

Eight

BETH SAT ON THE BED, her cellphone on speaker, looking out the window at the view of the Coachella Valley lights between her hotel room and the mountains in the distance. The full moon had just risen and painted the steep slopes a pinkish gray, and the setting sun far on the other side faintly backlit the stubble of pine trees way up at the top.

"How is ChiChi?" Beth asked, realizing at once that she should have asked her mother how she was first.

"Well, I'm fine and she's great," Ellen answered, a bit of snark in her voice. "She told me if you don't come back, she'll be happy to stay with me."

"You're spoiling her, aren't you?"

"Not a bit. She just knows she's loved here."

"You're not letting her on the furniture, are you? You know how much Dan hates it when she's on the furniture. I'm trying to teach her to stay on the floor."

"Oh, no," Ellen asserted. "I wouldn't do that."

"You're lying, Mother," Beth said, smiling at the mental image of her mother and ChiChi cuddling on the couch, her mother reading a thick historical novel, and the dog snoozing with her head on Ellen's lap. "I can hear it in your voice."

Ellen sighed loudly, a sound intended to get Beth off her back.

"Get off the couch, ChiChi!" Beth yelled into the phone. "Oh, that worked. Good girl, ChiChi," her mother intoned.

"She's still up there, isn't she?" Beth shook her head. It was a losing battle, but one she secretly liked losing. Just don't tell Dan, she thought.

"Yeah, she is. I don't know why Dan gets to decide who gets on your furniture or mine. It's not his house."

"No, but if we get married, it would be nice if ChiChi were trained right. It would cut down on the arguments," Beth said, wondering why she used the words "if we get married" instead of "when we get married." When had she started doing that?

"Honey, I don't think people should go into a marriage with thoughts of how to avoid arguments. It should be a joyous decision, not a strategic one."

"I don't want to talk about this now, Mother. We haven't set a date. I still have time to think about it."

"Well, how are the lessons going?"

Relieved at the change of topic, Beth's voice brightened. "Oh, great, Mom! Jake says I'm a natural!"

"Jake?"

"The instructor. He called me athletic. Imagine that! Me, an athlete?"

Her mother laughed loudly, and ChiChi barked. Clearly, the dog's ear was within inches of the phone.

"I'm not surprised. I always thought you were," her mother said. "And how is Dan doing?

"Oh, Jake kicked him out of the class." Beth knew it was an exaggeration, but it was the better story. "He wouldn't quit giving me tips. It was funny. You should have seen Dan's face. I don't think anyone has told Dan to get lost in a very long time."

"I kinda wish I'd been there," Ellen said.

"Yeah, you would've enjoyed it as much as I did."

THE NEXT MORNING THEY STOOD side by side, looking over the driving range shrouded with a low-hanging cloud, Beth wondered if Jake had dreamed as much about her as she had about him. He said nothing of the sort, of course, instead he pointed at the mountain tops poking up above the fog in the distance.

"You should be here when the snow covers those peaks," he said. "The bright white against that intense blue sky is magnificent."

"What, you're a poet too?" she teased.

"Clearly not. But I do think there is some magic to this valley. Not that I want to stay here forever, but I do try to appreciate what it offers as long as I'm here."

"Where would … " Beth started to ask, but as she turned to face him, she saw that he'd already picked up her bag and was headed over to the practice sand bunkers.

She shrugged. "Later, then." She followed him to the edge of a deep, sandy hole that lay right next to a smooth, lush green. Jake jumped down into the sand with one of her clubs in his hands. A couple dozen balls lay scattered at the bottom, and Jake raked one over to his feet.

"If there's one thing that's going to save your score in this game," he said, "it's getting out of the sand in one shot. You'd be surprised how many extra shots recreational golfers rack up because they never learn what to do in here."

Beth was amazed at how quickly he had shifted gears from mountain-gazing to serious instruction. She jumped into the sand, struggling to keep from falling against him.

"The keys to a great sand shot are simple," he said, "and few. But you can't resist them. You really can't do it any other way."

It sounded almost fascist, Beth thought. My way or the highway. But what did she know?

"Three things," Jake said, demonstrating. "You want to slap the sand two inches behind the ball. You want to turn the club face to the right and point your hips slightly to the left of the target—the hole." He pointed at the flagstick on the green. "And you want a very sharp up and down motion. Got it?"

"Slap sand, two inches behind the ball, open club, point the hips left, sharp up and sharp down," she repeated, as he hit another ball onto the green. "Sounds like six things, not three," she said, counting on her fingers.

Jake stopped chopping balls out of the sand and looked at her. "You are something," he said. "You are really something."

Beth put her hands on her hips and faked a frown. "What does that mean?" Was she flirting with him again? She needed to take this lesson seriously—it was expensive and time was short, after all—but the vibe between her and Jake kept interrupting her concentration.

Jake's eyes narrowed as if he were wondering the same thing—was she flirting and should he make her stop it? Finally, he shrugged and looked back down at the ball closest to his feet.

He demonstrated one more perfect shot, the ball obediently popping up and onto the green, and handed her the club. "Okay, now you try."

Beth pulled a ball up to her feet with the club and swatted at it, trying to imitate Jake. The ball skidded forward in the sand a couple of feet and stopped.

"Huh, not so easy," she muttered. She raked another

ball toward her, but Jake reached out and caught the shaft of her club.

"Wait," he said. "Which of those three things did you do?"

Beth stood up straight and thought for a moment. "None of them," she answered.

"Right. Most people think if they just jump into the sand and blast away, the ball will be so afraid of them it will hop right out of here. Not so."

"I wasn't thinking—"

"No, you weren't thinking," he scolded.

"You know, sometimes you tell me not to think, and sometimes you tell me I'm not thinking. I don't know what to do."

Jake just laughed.

"Now let's try again. And, yes, think this time."

A half-hour later, Beth was making some progress. About a quarter of the balls she hit ended up flying way over the green onto the driving range beyond. Another quarter never left the sand, but about half of them ended up on the putting surface, even if they stopped far from the hole.

Jake climbed out of the sand and reached a hand down to help her. She grabbed ahold and pulled herself up as he quickly backed away. He shouldered her bag and walked around the trap to the putting green, now dotted with the balls they hit out of the sand.

"Time for a putting lesson," he announced. He pulled out her putter and moved some balls around. He described and demonstrated his three keys to putting, and this time Beth didn't correct his count. She watched closely, and when he handed her the club, she focused on following his tips.

"Wait," he said, reaching in for the putter to stop her. "Let's look at your hands."

He stood behind her, much like he had twice before,

with his arms at her side. Viscerally aware of his body again, she caught her breath.

"You want to hold it lightly, like you're holding a baby bird," he said. "Relax. Here. Put your left hand here." He guided her hand onto the club. "And your right one here. And swing back and forth, keeping the club head square to the hole."

Beth could hardly hear him for the sound of her heart pounding in her ears. What was it about him that was doing this to her? She hadn't felt this way about Dan's presence for a long time. If ever? Jake stepped back a little, and she took a deep, shaky breath, closed and opened her eyes. She tried to move the club back and forth like he had. It wobbled.

Jake stepped close again and put his hands on top of hers. Together they swung the club back and forth, and then stopped. She turned her head to look at him and this time, Jake didn't move. His eyes moved to her lips, holding there for a moment, and then he let go.

"I am so sorry," Beth blurted. "I don't really mean to do that. You must think I'm really awful. Jesus, what if Dan …"

"No, no. It's my fault," Jake protested. He shook his head, turned, and walked away.

"I hardly think so." Beth shook her arms out and looked out across the driving range at the mountains. Should she say something about what was happening between them, or was it better left unsaid? Make an excuse? Try to defuse the tension?

"Look, I'm sure this happens to you all the time," she whispered at his back. "Let's just forget it," she said.

Jake stopped a few yards away and turned back toward her. He nodded, his grin a bit sheepish. "Yes. Let's do. Why don't you show me if you got the idea?"

He walked around in front of her to watch.

Beth took a deep breath, focused on the head of the

putter and swung it back and forth until the motion finally felt loose and easy. She stepped up to a ball, swung smoothly, and watched it drop in the hole.

"Bingo! See, you are a natural, just like I thought!" Jake said. "Why don't you hit a few more and then we'll stop early for lunch. Maybe we can sneak out about 11, between the early risers and the people who book the cheap greens fees after noon."

Nine

Instead of sitting in the outdoor café for lunch again, Jake suggested they grab a sandwich at the cantina and head directly out to the course. He had an appointment late in the afternoon, and Beth had promised she'd meet Dan about four o'clock for drinks at the pool bar.

As they drove out to the first tee box, Beth opened her hoagie and squirted some mustard out of the little foil packet onto the pastrami. She was surprised how all the sun and the exercise of swinging clubs had boosted her appetite. She usually had salads for lunch, but since she'd started taking lessons, a salad was not enough. She wanted bread and meat and cheese. And a slice of tomato, if it came along. A leaf of lettuce was okay but not necessary.

"There's something I wanted to ask you about," she said, after swallowing the first bite. "But maybe this isn't the right time."

Jake steered the cart with one hand and balanced the

wrapper for his hotdog on his lap. He had just taken a big bite. "Whaa??" he said, his mouth full of bun and dog.

Beth laughed. "Sorry," she said. "Go ahead and eat."

Jake nodded, chewed his mouthful, and pulled their cart up to the tee box. He took a swig from the huge diet soda that came with his dog and chips. "Now I'm good. What did you want to ask?"

"Maybe this is not the right time. I mean you may want to keep your distance from me. Outside of the lessons, I mean."

She paused, thinking about their near-embrace that morning and the one the afternoon before. Is that what she should call those close encounters? She wasn't sure. But now Jake was looking at her like she was nuts.

"I'm really sorry if I made it strange between us."

Jake scowled—not an angry grimace but a confused one. "Look, I don't want you to overthink this," he said.

"But weren't we just talking about how golf is really a mental game. Why wouldn't I overthink it?"

"Yes, I said that," Jake said, laughing. "But there's more to it than that. Golf isn't just brawn and brains and no feelings, but actually, it's a lot emotion. Why do you think a tour player wins a tournament one week and can't make the cut the next? It's not because he forgot how to swing a club or lost muscle tone. No. It's because his heart wasn't in it."

Beth smiled. It seemed they were at a point where they couldn't avoid talking about what they were experiencing. "Are you trying to say your heart is in this?" She pointed at him and then at herself with her sandwich.

Jake took another bite of his hotdog. Beth figured he was buying time as he tried to decide how to answer.

"Yeah, I guess that's what I'm saying." He looked ahead, down the cart path, as if afraid to meet her eyes. "Look. I really like you. But I understand you and Dan are—"

"Yes," she said, her voice dropping. "We are."

Jake shook his head. "Then I'm confused. What is it you wanted to ask me?"

"Well, it's really not that big a deal." How had they gotten off track so? She wasn't sure they were even talking about the same thing anymore. Or in the same language.

"Then out with it!"

"Okay," she said. "This is what I wanted to ask." She put her sandwich down on her seat, stepped out of the cart, pulled her five-wood out of her bag, and took a couple of practice swings while talking. "I know I'm not very good yet, but I think I'd like to get some real clubs. I mean clubs made for me. I just bought these off the shelf at a sporting goods store. They're not very good, are they?"

Jake let out a breath. He looked relieved. He pulled his driver from his bag and joined her on the tee box. "They're okay," he said. "But I agree. So, let me guess. You want me to help you pick something out?"

"Yeah."

"Oh, heavens. Is that all? I thought ... ." He shook his head and took a couple of practice swings.

"Let's do it!" he exclaimed. "Instead of golf tomorrow afternoon, let's grab lunch over by the golf store in Palm Desert and go shopping."

"Thanks. I didn't want to impose on you. I mean, I didn't know if I should ask you to go with me off this course."

Jake ignored that. "So, this afternoon, we'll play a few holes, and then I think we should quit early and do a rules lesson."

"Rules? What does that have to do with learning how to play golf?"

"Everything."

"But that doesn't sound like any fun."

"No, but rules keep the game fair. Buck it up, Beth. Everyone needs to learn them."

Dan pointed his club down the fairway. "It's time for

me to tee off," he said. "I can't hit far enough to reach that group on the green."

Beth looked where he was pointing. She couldn't see far enough to make out the group on the green, let alone hit far enough to reach them.

"Okay, let's go!"

She watched as Jake's ball flew high, straight and far, and felt a rush that she had to admit was pure animal attraction. How was she ever going to get over this thing between them if he kept swinging like that? She took a deep breath before she stepped up to the forward tee.

THE RULES LESSON TOOK ABOUT an hour, and by the time Jake had given her what he called "the basics," she was yawning. It wasn't so much that she was bored. It was more the heat of the day, combined with a big sandwich at lunch, and sitting still right after hours of physical activity.

"So, you think you have it now, sleepyhead?" he asked, his smile teasing.

"It all seems like too much to remember," she said, stifling another yawn.

"Well, it is. That's why you have a rules book." He pointed at the compact book he'd given her. "You can always look it up. But you can remember the basics. Don't ground your club in the bunkers. Play the ball as it lies. For the tougher stuff, like 'out of bounds' and 'line of sight,' look them up in the book."

"Does anyone know them all?"

"Only the rules officials. The men and women who officiate at tournaments. But let's drop this now. I have a few minutes before I have to leave, and I want to hear more about you. Tell me about yourself."

"Are you pretending that this is part of the lesson?" She leaned back and stretched her arms high over her head.

Jake looked at his watch. "No, lesson time is up. But I

have most of a beer and you have a full glass of wine. Don't want them to go to waste."

"So, what do you want to know?"

"Honestly," he whispered, leaning forward. "I'm very curious about you and Dan. You don't seem, well, can I say it? You don't seem perfect for each other."

"Well, I guess that's obvious to everyone but Dan." She wasn't sure she wanted to share more. There had already been too many awkward moments between her and Jake on the course. She could imagine how sharing her ambivalence about Dan could make things worse.

Or better.

"How did you meet?" Jake was clearly not going to give up until he got some answers.

"Okay. I'll give you the abridged version," she said. "At my last job, I was assigned to a company event at Amazon where he works. I always thought of Amazon as full of young guys, you know. Bachelors. Techies. Making lots of money and not very interested in meeting women. But it was a company picnic, and for some reason, it seemed like all families. Dan was obviously alone, and he works with a guy who dates a friend of mine. He came by the table where I was managing the food service, and we started talking. I had no idea then that his passion was golf and that he hated dogs, or it would never have gone anywhere."

"But it did."

Beth smiled sadly. "Yes. I guess it's one of those bad habits that gets so engrained you can't shake it."

"Bad habit? I never heard anybody talk about their relationship like that."

"Obviously, an overstatement. Really, I like him a lot. When he's not on the golf course, he can be a lot nicer."

"So you're a caterer or something?

"I'm an event planner, actually. At least that was my job. I'm between jobs now, as they say in polite company. In the pandemic, the catering business I was working for went under. So, I'm looking. I had an interview at Starbucks before we left, and I'm hoping I'll land there when we get back."

"Did you ever think of moving to the desert? Get out of the rain?"

Beth grinned. "Why? Would that matter to you in some way?" she teased.

"Well, maybe someday I'll need a caterer," Jake said. He shrugged as if to say "you never know."

Beth chuckled. "You know, I really like you, too."

"You think that's what I was saying?"

"Was it?"

Jake held her eyes for a few moments, his smile fading. "Yes. I guess it was."

"But you must meet a thousand women out here on the driving range." She gestured toward the lesson area down the slope.

Jake nodded. "I do. Yes, I do."

"Do you ask all of them if they want to move to the desert?"

That made him laugh. "Boy, you are tough, Beth. Good questions. You should be a TV reporter."

She stuck her fist out toward his face as if she held a microphone. "And your answer?"

"I'm afraid this isn't going to help," he said, serious all of the sudden. "Never. Honestly, I have never asked anyone that before."

Beth couldn't miss his expression. It was a cross between bewildered and sad. She took a deep breath. "Well, then, I suppose I owe you a serious answer. I couldn't live here. It's too hot. And the sun shines all of the time."

Jake laughed. "Only someone from Seattle would complain about too much sun! You love your rain."

"Actually," she countered, "we're a bit ambivalent about the rain. We like it; we're used to it; we brag about it. But even for us, a sun break now and then is awfully nice."

Jake looked up over her head toward the entrance to the patio. Beth turned to follow his eyes. Dan walked toward them, and he didn't look pleased.

"So, what's going on here? I thought we were meeting at the tiki bar at four?"

"Oh! I didn't realize how late it was," she said. "Jake was just giving me a rules lesson." She held up the rules book Jake had given her.

"Look, man, I'm sorry," Jake interjected. "I lost track of time."

Dan answered him with a scowl. "Sure. I'm sure you did," he said, and turned back to Beth. "Come on. Let's go. I'm thirsty and hungry."

Jake stood up and threw a twenty-dollar bill on the table. "See you tomorrow morning, Beth."

He bowed slightly to Dan. "Enjoy your date."

Ten

BETH ARRIVED AT THE ROPED-OFF lesson area of the driving range the next morning before Jake for the first time. She was diligently following the stretching routine he had taught her when he scampered down the hill toward her.

"Sorry." He was breathing heavily, having apparently run some distance to get there. "My car is in the shop, and I had to walk over."

"Walk?" Beth laughed. "It looks like you ran the whole way." She continued to warm up, now swinging a couple of clubs like baseball bats, a drill to build upper body strength.

Jake watched her as he caught his breath. Two days earlier, his gaze would have been intimidating, but now, she was getting used to his scrutiny. She hoped it would eventually help her get over the jitters she always felt when strangers watched her on the tee box.

"Are we going to go shopping today?" he asked. "Is it okay with Dan?"

Beth stopped swinging. "But if you don't have a car …."

"Oh, don't worry. The shop is delivering it to the parking lot here mid-morning," he said. "I'm really looking forward to helping you find new clubs."

"Great." She put her clubs back in the bag. "What are we working on this morning?"

"Uhhh …,"Jake pinched his lips together and scratched the back of his head. He looked like he wanted to say something but didn't know how.

"What? Is there something wrong?"

"I just need to say I'm sorry about yesterday afternoon."

"Sorry for what?"

"For keeping you late. I'm not sure I did your relationship with Dan any favors."

Beth waved his words away. "Oh, don't be sorry. And don't mind Dan. For a guy who is certain that I should marry him, he sure seems insecure, doesn't he?"

"You think he thought … ?"

"Oh, yeah. He always thinks …" She shrugged.

"It must get tiring."

She shrugged again. "Well, I guess the good thing is he really cares."

"About you or about getting married?"

Beth squinted at him. He had just summed up her dilemma, hadn't he? Was Dan just committed to getting married and fitting in with his Amazon colleagues? Or was he committed to marrying her? She decided it was a question better left unanswered for the moment.

"We're here for a lesson, right, Jake? What are we going to work on today?"

"Right," Jake smirked, making fun of his distraction. "You're right. I think we should work on pitching and chipping. The short game is more important than most people realize."

He picked up her bag and pointed toward the sand trap

and green of the short-game practice area. "Let's go over there and get started."

By lunch hour, Jake appeared to have shed whatever concerns he'd brought to the morning session, and Beth relaxed. She didn't want the good rapport they had built—or maybe it was even more than that—stifled by Dan's poor attitude. After grabbing a sandwich for the road, Jake drove them down to the PGA Superstore on Highway 111, the main artery through town.

Beth was at a loss as she followed him down the aisles of Ping, Callaway, Tour Edge, Titleist, Cleveland, Taylor-Made, and Cobra club sets. It seemed like he was just wandering through the displays, looking randomly at different brands. Did he have some parameters in mind as he considered them?

Finally, he stopped and waved for her to catch up with him. "Here. Come here, Beth. I think this would be a good choice for you. It has a fairly forgiving club head design, but it will work for you for a long time. And we can order them totally custom for your height and swing speed."

Beth pulled one of the woods out of its slot in the display and waggled it close to the ground. She didn't have any idea what she was looking for, but she was fairly sure that what the club looked like didn't rank high among the selection criteria.

"Can I try them?" she asked.

"Absolutely. In fact, you must." Jake pulled a couple of irons and a hybrid out of the slots. "Follow me."

With the iron still in her hands, she followed him toward the big, tented area where people were hitting balls off of artificial turf mats into stiff tarps about twenty yards away. Jake took the club she carried and handed all of them to an attendant standing at the front of an empty bay. The guy looked like a pro linebacker—big, wide-shouldered, and square-jawed. A bit intimidating, but with a quick smile.

"Jake, you old snake!" The big man laughed. "Found a new victim, have you?"

Jake and the man shared a quick one-armed man-hug.

"Brian, this is Beth. One of the quickest studies I've ever had the pleasure of coaching," Jake said. "She's looking to buy her first custom clubs."

Jake turned to her. "Brian and I go way back, back to our college days at ASU. He helped me get the job at the resort."

Brian leaned the clubs against a bag stand. "What do you have here?" He picked up one of the irons and swung it. "A bit advanced for a beginner, don't you think?"

"I told you, she's got potential. I want her to have clubs she can grow into."

"Hmm." Brian nodded. "Well, then seems like a good choice. We can customize them, fit them with a lighter shaft."

"That's what I told her. She wants to take a few swings."

Brian put some tape over the club faces and handed the shortest iron to Beth.

"Step up to the plate, lady, and let's see what you've got." Brian pointed at the square green mat.

"Boy, you really know how to put a girl on the spot, don't you?" Beth frowned at Brian.

"Just ignore him," Jake said. "You have a better swing than he does."

Beth grimaced. She stepped onto the mat and took a quick practice swing. Realizing it was a poor, rushed effort, she took a deep breath and took a long, easy swing, just like Jake had taught her. Then she raked a ball into place, looked at her target—the middle of the tarp—took another deep breath, relaxed her shoulders, and tried to execute a swing she could be proud of. The ball arced nicely and struck the tarp right where she intended.

She turned and looked at Jake for his reaction.

"Nice swing, Beth," Brian said. He sounded sincere.

Jake elbowed him. "I told you. She has learned all of this in just a few days."

"A natural," Brian said.

"Yup." Jake's grin was bigger than her own.

Brian looked at her with a serious face. "Be careful, my dear," he whispered harshly. "I think your instructor is a bit infatuated."

Beth tried to wipe the smile off her face, but it wouldn't move. More confident now, she raked another ball into place and took another easy shot. She watched it hit the target and turned to Brian and winked.

"Can you blame him?"

Eleven

As the host led Beth and Dan to a table far back in a dark corner of the fancy steakhouse Dan had chosen for dinner that evening, she made herself a promise. She was going to say nothing that increased Dan's insecurities and say as many things as she could to wipe away any suspicions he might harbor about Jake. The afternoon shopping trip made her face up to what she hadn't accepted yet: that Jake was as smitten as she was, and it was up to her to stop it. A relationship with a golf instructor wasn't a real thing. It was the plot of a silly romance novel.

"Well, this is nice and cozy," Dan said, as they sat. He nodded his appreciation to the host. "Isn't this just perfect?" he asked Beth.

"Yes, lovely. But it seems like such a waste to not be outside as much as we can while we're here. We'll be back in the rain soon enough. At least we should be sitting at a window."

Dan rolled his eyes and his face sunk into a pout. "Here I thought I'd done something right for a change," he said.

Already! Already she had said the wrong thing. Beth stomped the heel of one of her shoes on the toe of the other to punish herself.

"No, no!" she said, reaching across the table for his hand. "Of course, this is perfect. I guess I'm realizing we have only five more days here, and I'm wishing it were more like five more weeks."

"Yes, me too. But right now, I'm starved. Golf can really work up an appetite."

"Yes, it does."

"So, you're enjoying your lessons? Are you learning anything?"

"Funny you should ask. Jake says—" She caught herself. No more mention of Jake! "I'm hitting the ball much better. I'm more relaxed. Maybe I'm an athlete after all."

Dan opened the wine list. "Really?" he said, studying the offerings. "I've never thought of you as athletic. Brainy, yes. Beautiful, without a doubt. But not athletic."

Beth was ready to chastise him for thinking so narrowly of her, but she caught herself. "I used to play tennis. Remember?" she said instead.

"Oh, yeah," he answered, not looking up from the menu. "I never really liked tennis."

"Right." Beth watched him peruse the list for a minute. She focused on his face, how handsome it was. She thought about how much he wanted to marry her, how successful he was. These were good things. These were worth hanging on to. Whatever her reservations were, she needed to keep her head on her shoulders and not let her foolish infatuation with a golf instructor sway her judgment.

"But I'm starting to see what you like about golf," she said as he put down the menu and looked up.

"That's great! Because there's something I would like to

propose tonight. I've been thinking about it all day."

"What's that?" Beth's heart skipped. Was he going to push for a wedding date again?

"Let's wait until we get some champagne in front of us," Dan said, flagging down the waiter.

"Sure." She forced the word out.

Dan pointed to a line on the menu, the waiter nodded, and walked away.

"How did you play today?" she asked.

"Great. Ryan and George are a hoot."

"They played with you again today?"

"Yup. And tomorrow." Dan looked the happiest he had all week.

"How is it they can play every day?"

"They have some sort of membership cards. They get a discount."

Beth shook her head. "No, I meant, don't they work anymore? You said George worked in L.A."

"Used to. I get the feeling they come from money. You know. Trust funders, maybe?"

"Ah." She nodded. They opened their dinner menus and bent their heads to study them. The waiter arrived with an uncorked champagne bottle in a bucket of ice on a stand and set it by the table. He lifted the bottle.

"Sir, would you like to taste?"

"Nah," said Dan. "Just pour."

Once the waiter completed pouring and left, Dan lifted his flute toward her, and Beth obliged, touching her glass to his. She sipped. Another thing to appreciate, she thought. Dan was a guy who could afford a great vintage like this.

"Before we get to what you wanted to say over champagne," she said. "I'd like to ask you something."

Dan nodded, and she continued. "Do you think it's a good idea if I get some clubs made?"

"You mean custom clubs?"

"Yeah. Jake took me to the Superstore today, and this guy, Brian, he helped me figure out what I should get." She figured if Dan thought some stranger named Brian was involved, and not just Jake, he might put up less resistance to the idea.

To her surprise, he looked pleased.

"I think it's a great idea," he said with enthusiasm. "You should order them. I'll get them for you as an early wedding present."

Beth hadn't thought much about how she would pay for them. In a way, they would be a good wedding gift, cementing their new, shared pastime. On the other hand, would that be another way he could force a quick wedding?

"Or, if you can pay for them," she suggested, "I can pay you back as soon as I get a job."

"Whatever," he said. "But this is a perfect segue to what I wanted to ask."

He took another sip of champagne. Fortification? she wondered. How bad was this request going to be?

"Okay, I'll just out with it," he said. "I was thinking since you've taken to golf so well, maybe you'd be willing to make our honeymoon a golf trip. Maybe Hawaii? Or even New Zealand?"

Beth realized she wasn't going to be able to avoid the wedding discussion. She tried to smile.

"Dan, we haven't even set a wedding date yet. How can you be talking about the honeymoon?"

"Well, that's just it. I'm thinking if we want to plan the perfect golf honeymoon, we need to plan ahead. It's not easy to get reservations at some of the best resorts. If we choose where we want to go for our honeymoon, then we'll know what time of year we should go, and it will help us set a wedding date." He looked immensely pleased with his logic.

"That seems sort of upside down or backwards, doesn't

it?" She had intended to avoid arguing with him over dinner, but here it was. The same old dispute, just a different approach.

The waiter arrived, giving them a respite for a moment. After they ordered and the waiter left, Dan looked just as disappointed as she expected he would.

"Okay, you tell me how we decide this thing," he said. "I've been waiting a year for you to agree to a date. Nothing seems to move you forward."

Beth nodded. "I'm sorry, but I just don't understand the hurry. What's the rush?"

"Look. Everyone I know is married. I feel like the loser at work. They all talk about their kids and their family vacations. We've been dating three years now, and no one believes me when I say we're engaged."

So that was it! "Is that a reason to get married? Everyone else is doing it? To prove something to your co-workers?" Beth asked.

Dan closed his eyes and squeezed them together with a thumb and finger. "No, of course not. But we should get married because we're in love. That's what people in love do." When he looked at her again, his eyes were pleading.

"Right" was all she could think to say.

"I'm beginning to wonder if you want to get married."

"Someday, yes," she answered. But that didn't change Dan's worried face. "No, of course I do," she assured him hurriedly. She sighed. "How about we say a year from now. Next November?"

Dan's face immediately brightened. "Okay! Great!" He lifted he glass again. "Now we have something to celebrate!"

He put his glass down and squinted as he thought. "If it's November, how about New Zealand?" he asked. "Or Australia? It's summer down there."

"Sure, honey," Beth said, trying to hide the resignation in her voice. "Either one."

Twelve

By the end of her lesson Monday morning, Beth was starting to feel like a golfer. Like someone who could play the game with anyone. Sure, she'd never outscore Dan, but she could hit the ball reliably down the fairway, she knew what club to use given where her ball lay, and she had figured out how to hit a ball out of the sand on the first shot at least half the time.

"Maybe I really can do this," she said. "Maybe I can really play golf someday."

"You already can," Jake said. She looked up. She hadn't realized she'd said her thought out loud. She grimaced but Jake was smiling.

"Just think," he said. "Four days in and you're hitting balls like you've been playing for years."

"Well, months, maybe."

Jake nodded. "Yeah, months. But just wait 'til you get those new clubs. Did you talk with Dan about them?"

"Yes. He said he'd get them for me as an early wedding present."

Jake looked away. When he returned his gaze to her, he'd forced what was obviously a fake smile.

"Well, that's wonderful. I'll call Brian and have him order them. Let's go catch some lunch and get out on the course. They're predicting some rain this afternoon, and I'd like us to get at least nine holes in."

"Okay." Beth was happy. Although it made little sense, it was a relief to have finally settled on a wedding month. The pressure was off. She'd agreed with Dan, and now she believed all her ambiguity and uncertainly would disappear. Instead of making her feel more trapped, the decision freed her from worrying about it.

Jake chose a table for them at the edge of the patio. From there, they could watch golfers on the eighteenth green shake hands and climb into their carts at the end of their rounds. The temperature had dropped a few degrees, and the pleasant weather added to Beth's good mood. It seemed to rub off on Jake, and before their food was placed before them, he had loosened up. Perhaps having the question of Beth's marriage settled was helping him too.

Wanting to retain their good spirits, she asked him tell stories of his professional career. Other than his reason for leaving the tour, he'd told her nothing about it. It turned out he had a great sense for storytelling, and even though his time on the tour hadn't been particularly successful, it hadn't killed his sense of humor.

He told her about a time when he slipped on the mud into an alligator-infested swampy slough in Florida and surfacing to face a mouth full of giant teeth.

"All I could think about was 'where is my pitching wedge?'" he finished, guffawing at the memory. "This monster was about to bite me in half, and I was worried about a hundred-dollar golf club!"

Beth laughed so hard she had tears in her eyes. Bending toward him and putting her head against his shoulder, she tried to catch her breath. "I can just see you in there, covered in green slime!" As she lifted her head and took a deep breath, she looked out toward the course.

"Oh, no!" she said, suddenly serious. Jake turned his head to follow her eyes.

Dan stood with two other golfers just beyond the ledge that divided the patio from the grass around it. He was looking right at her, his angry eyes telling her that he had just watched her place her head against Jake's arm. Did he see their joy? Their companionship? Did he feel excluded?

"Oh, no is right." Jake turned back to face her and whispered. "That's George with him, isn't it?"

"Yeah, I guess," she said. "But I don't know what difference that makes. I'm already in trouble."

"It might be worse than you think," Jake said. He looked apologetic. "I'm sorry. I think this could be difficult."

The only way to make things look better, Beth decided quickly, was to act like nothing had happened. She smiled and waved cheerfully at Dan. "Hi, honey," she called out.

Dan scowled and shook his head before walking away. The two men with him stared at Beth and Jake a little longer, and then turned and followed him.

Early that evening, Beth sat with Dan and his friends at a high-top in a hamburger joint that Ryan and George said was the best in the whole Coachella Valley. What made it so great, Beth surmised, was the number of huge TVs that hung from the ceiling behind the bar and all the way around the dining area. The roar of the Monday Night Football broadcast blasted out of at least a dozen big, black speakers.

When they had driven from the hotel to the restaurant, Dan didn't mention that he'd seen her on the patio at the golf course with Jake. Either what he saw didn't bother him as much as she expected, or he was saving his reaction for a later time. Beth had no way to know and she was too afraid of the argument it could engender to bring it up.

Likewise, Ryan and George greeted her and acted as if they hadn't seen her and Jake either. As she shook their hands and then hopped up onto the barstool, they looked her over as if they'd never seen her before. Or maybe, she thought, that was just the shameless way they looked at all women.

"So, what do you do up there in Seattle?" George asked as she helped herself to a glass of beer from one of the two half-full pitchers in the middle of the table.

"I'm between jobs, but I set up events for corporations," she said. "You know, things like investor meetings, new product launches, employee meetings, picnics."

It all either went over George's head or he hadn't really been interested in an answer. He turned immediately back to the football game on the TV right above them and took a big gulp of beer. Without turning away from the game, he asked a question she figured was really closer to what he wanted to know. "So, how are your golf lessons going?"

"Okay," she said. She glanced up to see what football action had all the men so rapt. The referees in their black and white-striped shirts were huddled, and the announcer was speculating about what penalty was being discussed. It seemed a bit silly to spend so much energy trying to guess when the answer would be divulged in less than a minute. But then, she never really understood the devotion football fans had for the announcers—male or female. She knew women who were just as riveted by the play-by-play and penalties as Dan and his friends were.

"I think I might take to this game after all," she said, completing her thought.

"Football?" Ryan asked. "Well, why not. Greatest game on earth, other than golf, of course."

George slugged his friend in the shoulder. "She's talking about golf, dodo," he said. The penalty finally revealed on the TV, he turned back to her. "And what do you think of Jake?"

She expected the question, but out of the corner of her eye, she saw Dan shaking his head and pumping the palm of his hand downward. It was his "tone it down" signal.

She turned to catch Dan's eyes, but he quickly focused on the TV again.

"Well," she answered George. "I don't know much. He's the first instructor I've ever had. How will I know if he's any good?"

"But he's charming right?"

This time, Dan didn't even try to hide his frustration with George. He rolled his eyes and buried his forehead in his hands.

"Did you put him up to this?" Beth asked her fiancé. "Is this some kind of test?"

"Should it be?" George asked.

"George!" Dan bellowed. "Lay off. Really."

"Of course, you did," she said, speaking to Dan. "Why don't you ask me what you really want to know? Too afraid of the answer?"

Dan looked frightened and tongue-tied. If he had planned this inquisition, it wasn't going well. But then he was saved by Beth's ringing phone. She picked it up and looked at the caller ID.

"Sorry, guys," she said, sarcastically. "I'd love to continue this line of questioning, but I have to take this."

She jumped down from her stool and walked outside.

"Hey, Debra," she answered. "What's up?"

"I've been trying to reach you all day," her friend at Starbucks said. "Aren't you looking at messages?"

"Oh," Beth realized she hadn't thought about checking her phone all day. "No, I guess not."

"Well, then you must be having fun."

"A blast," Beth said. "I'm really catching onto this golf thing."

"I'll bet Dan is pleased."

"Well, yes and no. I'll explain it all later. Bottom line is that I haven't been playing with him."

The line went silent for a few moments. Beth guessed that Deb was trying to figure out what that meant. "Then, who are you playing with?" Deb finally asked.

"My instructor."

"Good looking?"

Beth shook her head. Was that all women thought about? How men looked? But maybe turn-around was fair play.

"I haven't noticed," she lied.

"Liar." Beth laughed heartily. "But I'll wait till you get back for details."

"I promise I'll tell you everything. But why'd you call? What's up? Are you still in the office?"

"Yes, but everyone else is gone, so I figured I could call you and give you the good news. The hiring manager for that position you interviewed for? She called me today to talk about you. It's sounding good, Beth. I thought you'd like to know."

"Yay!" Beth had nearly forgotten about the interview, but now she was excited again. "That's great news. What'd she ask you?"

"The usual. 'The right fit' kind of stuff. I told her you'd be great. So, anyway, I thought you should probably keep an ear open for your phone. She might be calling soon to offer you the job."

Behind her, Beth heard Dan open the restaurant door. She turned to see him peeking out.

"Who are you talking to?" he asked. He sounded irritated. "We're going to order food."

"Hold on a second," Beth said into the phone and pulled it away from her face. "It's Debra," she told Dan. "She has good news about the Starbucks job." She waved him away. "I'll be right there."

Dan went back inside, and Beth put the phone back to her ear. "I've got to go Deb. We're having hamburgers with Dan's new golf buddies. I guess they're missing me."

"You're so popular! Okay. Call me if you hear anything."

Thirteen

A COUPLE OF HOURS LATER, the football game over and un-impressive hamburgers ordered and consumed, Beth sat at the hotel bar with Dan, expecting them to finally talk about what he saw at lunch. He'd ordered a martini, but instead of drinking it, he was staring off in the distance and scowling. He appeared reluctant to start the conversation.

She wanted to get it over with.

"I thought you were happy that I was getting into golf," she said.

"I am. I just think maybe you're spending a lot of time with Jake," he said. For a guy who just spent a couple of hours drinking beer with his new best buddies, he sure was in a foul mood.

"Yes, I am," she said. "Yes, I am. You paid for lessons and backed out of them. I'm taking them. You are playing golf, and I don't complain that you're spending a lot of time with George and Ryan."

Dan said nothing, so Beth continued. "Anyway, does this concern of yours have anything to do with George?"

"What?"

"Come on. That third degree he was trying to give me at dinner. He was grilling me about Jake."

"No. Okay. Kinda." Dan tipped his martini up and swallowed it in one gulp. That was unlike him. He'd never been a drinker. "Jake stole George's girlfriend."

Beth laughed and then caught herself when she saw Dan's horrified expression.

"Are you serious?" she asked. "No one 'steals' someone else's girlfriend. What do you think women are? Objects on a shelf that someone can shoplift? If George's girlfriend left him for Jake, I can't say I'm surprised."

Dan shook his glass at the bartender who nodded and started to mix another one.

"I just don't think you should be having lunch with him anymore," Dan said. He was dead serious.

"You've got to be kidding," Beth said. Now she was getting angry. This was so silly. "What? Are you jealous? This is ridiculous."

"If he's making moves on you, you aren't the first. He does this all the time. Don't think you're special. He's just doing what he does. All the time."

"This is insane." Beth lowered her voice to a harsh whisper. "You don't trust me. Is that it?"

Dan accepted his fresh martini with a nod. "No, I don't trust him."

"So, who am I supposed to have lunch with? Or do you think I should just have lunch by myself?"

"I'll meet you for lunch tomorrow," Dan said, as if he had been wanting to do that all along. He'd never mentioned it before. "We're playing a second eighteen in the afternoon, but we'll take a break after the first round and I'll meet you on the patio."

"How big of you." Beth smirked. "Are you sure George and Ryan won't be jealous?" She stood up, slammed a ten-dollar bill on the bar and left her own martini untouched. "I'm going to bed."

Dan didn't lift his chin from the bar as she walked away.

SITTING ON THE PATIO THE next day, Beth looked at her watch again. It was almost one o'clock, and she'd been waiting for Dan for forty-five minutes. In another ten, she had to meet Jake for their afternoon round on the course. Her phone buzzed.

"Well, it's about time." She scowled.

She picked it up. A text from Dan:

I'm sorry I'm late. Be there in a minute.

She waited another five minutes and gave up. She hadn't ordered lunch, as she expected to eat with him. She laid down a five-dollar bill to pay for her iced tea and to somewhat compensate for taking up a table for nearly an hour, and started to walk to the entrance. Putting her billfold back in her backpack, she nearly ran into Dan.

"Honey, I'm so sorry," he said. He held her shoulders and huffed breathlessly. "We had a frost delay, and we got a late start. I tried to hurry, but the course was really backed up."

"Terrific, Dan," she said, nearly spitting her words. "You don't trust me to have lunch with my golf instructor, and this is your solution."

He shrugged, and it occurred to Beth that she'd seen a lot of that on this vacation. For a man with such high self-esteem and such authority at work, he had turned into quite a wimp out here in the desert.

"Is this going to be what happens on our golf honeymoon?" she asked. "You take off with the boys, and I get to have lunch by myself? Sounds wonderful. I can't wait."

She tried to walk around him. He caught her arm.

"No, stay," he begged. "I want to have lunch with you."

She shook off his grasp. "Too late, Dan. My lesson starts up again in five minutes. With Jake. Maybe you can get George and Ryan to join you."

Four holes into their afternoon practice round, Beth was ready to give up. She'd not driven well from any of the tee boxes, and her fairway shot on the fourth hole barely left the ground, spitting straight off to the right at about a 90-degree angle from where she was aiming.

All afternoon, Jake had let Beth fume and swear without remark. That he could read her so well floated in the back of her mind. If he had commented on every shot—good and bad—her temper would have boiled over. This was one of those times when it was best for everyone to leave her alone, and Jake must have sensed that.

But after the horrid shank she had just produced, he stepped up beside her and picked up the club she had thrown on the ground.

"What do you think happened there?" he said, looking over at the ball resting in the brown rough.

"I don't know." Beth moaned. "I lifted up?"

"Yes, think about keeping your head steady—"

Beth turned away and walked to the cart without listening. She sat down hard and crossed her arms over her chest. "You know what, Jake. I don't care. I never wanted to learn how to play this stupid game in the first place."

Jake slipped her club into her bag and steered the cart over to collect her errant ball.

"What's wrong this afternoon?" he asked, his voice low.

"What isn't wrong?" Beth was angry enough to cry, but she wasn't going to embarrass herself with tears over Dan's behavior. "I hate this game."

Jake pulled the cart up to her ball and stepped out to retrieve it, while she sat, stubborn, her arms still crossed.

Instead of steering back to his ball in the middle of the fairway, he turned the cart and headed back toward the clubhouse.

"You know what I think?" he said. "I think we've had too much golf. I have an idea. Mind if we get out of here for a couple of hours?"

"Pfftt." Beth stewed. "I really don't care."

With the cart accelerator floored, Jake whipped up to the door of the cart barn. "I know just what we need," he said.

He grabbed Beth by the hand, pulled her out of the cart, and headed toward the parking lot with her in tow.

"But my clubs ... ," she protested.

"Don't worry. The guys will take care of them for us," he said. "Come on. We're going to have some fun."

Ten miles away and forty minutes later, Beth and Jake were winding up a ferociously contested game of putt-putt. The silly windmill, clown's mouth, and troll's tunnel wiped away Beth's rage and took her mind off anything serious— like marrying Dan. Especially marrying Dan.

Lining up to take a putt on the final hole, Beth stopped and looked up at Jake.

"Thanks," she said, her smile sheepish. "I needed this. You knew just what to do."

"Yeah, well," he said motioning at her putter. "Hurry up and putt. I'm thirsty and I have just the spot picked out for our next stop."

Beth laughed and stood looking at him for a few more seconds before whacking at the ball and watching it spin a 360 around the hole before it dropped in.

Later, as she sank into a comfortable barstool at an outside bar not far from the miniature golf course, she raised her skinny can of hard seltzer to his beer for a toast.

"Wow, that was fun," she exclaimed. "What a great thing to do."

"My pleasure." Jake was all smiles.

"You're a lot of fun," she said.

"You are too."

"No, I mean that was just what I needed. And you knew it."

"And Dan wouldn't?"

Beth shook her head. "I don't want to talk about Dan anymore. Not today, okay?"

That seemed to cheer Jake up even more. "Absolutely," he said. "Why don't you tell me more about what you do— that catering thing. I think it might be something I could use."

"Okay," Beth said, surprised at his choice of topic. "Well, I manage events. I arrange everything from the sound system to the flowers to the food to the wait staff to the venue. I'm really good at it. I'm really organized."

"I'll bet you are. Maybe you can help me find someone like that."

"Why would you need someone like that?"

Jake took a big swig of beer. He looked a bit hesitant, and she encouraged him to answer with a circular wave of her hand.

"Here it is," he said. "I'd like to start my own golf school. I could easily find three or four other instructors to join me. There are plenty of unemployed PGA instructors around—just about everywhere. But I know nothing about setting up venues and figuring out the logistics. You know, lodging, meals and stuff."

"Doesn't it take a lot of money to do that? I mean for marketing and renting driving ranges and the stuff?"

Jake nodded. "I did make some money on the tour. Not a lot, but I live pretty cheaply, and I have some savings."

Beth considered what it would require to organize a golf school that wasn't sponsored by a golf resort like the one she was attending. It wouldn't take long to figure it out. A few phone calls, a spreadsheet, a review of golf school marketing materials. But he was asking her to help him find someone, not to do it herself.

"I'll check around with people I know and see who I can recommend," she said. "Most event planners do weddings, but there's a few like me who stay away from bridezillas."

Jake laughed. "You seem to have a fairly broad disdain for weddings," he said. "But thanks. Anything you can tell me would be great."

They fell into a companionable silence. Beth lifted her head to the slight, dry breeze that blew across the patio and stared out at the mountains.

"You want to talk about it?" Jake said. Beth frowned, trying to understand his question.

"About what?"

"Well, things seemed fine this morning on the driving range. But you came back from lunch upset."

Beth turned away from his eyes. "Dan stood me up for lunch," she muttered.

"Frost delay?"

"Yeah. How'd you know?"

"It was posted in the clubhouse this morning."

"Why didn't you tell me?"

Jake smiled crookedly. "I didn't know what your plans were. You just told me you were busy at noon and couldn't eat with me. You didn't tell me why."

Beth acknowledged the fact with a nod. "So, Dan shows up an hour late."

"I'd never do that."

Beth ignored that. It was easy for him to say, but it was unlikely that he would need to prove it in her lifetime. She searched his eyes for sincerity. If she was reading him right, he was offering himself up as an alternative to Dan. But was this real, or was this just a golf instructor thing, like George had suggested?

She breathed deep for courage and plunged in. "Do you know George?" she asked.

"You mean George as in George and Ryan, the Bobbsey Twins?" He sneered. "Sure, I know George. Is that who Dan played with this morning."

"Every day. And George has apparently convinced Dan that you are one dangerous dude, out to steal every man's woman."

"I'm not surprised," Jake said, nearly under his breath.

"Want to tell me what happened?"

Jake shook his head. "You know, I really don't. All I can say is it wasn't whatever George thought it was."

"That doesn't surprise me." She finished her seltzer and motioned to the bartender for another. "But you know ..." she paused. She wasn't sure she wanted to continue. "You know what happened the other day? Between us? On that putting green? And the day before on the fairway?"

"So I suppose George told you I do that all the time," he said, sardonically. He was hurt. "Any chance I get, I trap women on the putting green between my arms."

Beth put her hand on Jake's forearm and squeezed it lightly. "I don't care what George told me. But I do wonder. Does this happen to you all the time? Or is there something special here?"

"You mean between us?

Exasperation seeped from Jake's lips. He looked away. "It doesn't matter, Beth. You're getting married. You're planning your honeymoon. What difference does it make how I feel about you? I've only known you for a few days, and you're leaving in a couple more. Our last lesson together is tomorrow morning. It's not even a full day."

She was as sad as he was, she realized. She had felt warm and happy with his arms along hers. She loved the way being outdoors and laughing with her seemed like enough for him. He didn't need to prove—any more than she did—that he was marriageable, could settle down and make a family, could make a million dollars a year in stock options. Those were Dan's measures. Not hers. And apparently not Jake's.

And now she'd accused Jake of something she shouldn't even have listened to.

"I'm sorry," she said. She held up her left hand. "But see? No ring. Things could change, Jake. If I knew for sure how you felt about me, maybe things could change. Maybe the desert wouldn't be so bad for me. But I'd have to know if we'd have a chance ..."

She was stopped by Jake's face. He didn't just like her. She knew it was more than that. And while she had vowed to stop encouraging him, her feelings overrode her resolve. She held her breath, and they held each other's gaze. As he leaned toward her, she closed her eyes. His lips were warm and full, and she let herself sink into them.

Then her phone rang, startling them both. They quickly jerked apart, and Beth looked at the screen.

"Oh! This is the call I was waiting for." She looked at Jake apologetically. "Can you hold on a just a second?" She stood up and walked a few feet away. She listened and nodded.

"Yes! Yes, of course. I can start next Monday. That will be great."

She looked over to see Jake's smile fall away. "I'll see you then," she said and hung up.

"That was the call! I got the job!" she said, sliding back onto her bar stool.

Jake stared at his beer and said nothing. Beth nudged him with her elbow. "Isn't that good news?"

He shrugged. Then he looked up and forced a smile. "Congratulations, Beth. I'm sure you'll be great at it."

He stood up and pulled a few bills out of his wallet. "We should go. You have a lot to get ready for. I won't hold you to your last lesson. Maybe you should get back to Seattle as soon as you can."

Beth reached out to stop him. "But I don't want us to end it like this." At least she didn't think she did. But would it be better to stop this flirtation before it got deeper, harder to pull away from?

Jake answered for her. "You have to go back to Seattle. It's probably better now than …" He started to walk away. She jumped down and followed him.

"Our timing sucks. We could have …"

She couldn't figure out what more she could say. They walked to his car.

Fourteen

JAKE PULLED UP TO THE hotel portico and waited for Beth to get out, but she didn't move, unable to figure out what to say.

"Look," Jake said without looking over at her. "Let's not belabor this. You need to get back to Seattle. I've got another client starting tomorrow afternoon. We should just say goodbye now."

Hurt by his sudden frostiness but understanding his disappointment, Beth nodded. "Okay. I guess you're right. Goodbye, Jake." She leaned over the console, brushed her lips against his cheek, and got out of the car.

He drove away without looking back. Finally, as he disappeared around a corner, she turned and walked into the lobby.

She was digging in her backpack for her room key when Dan suddenly stood in front of her, holding a dozen huge roses. He was wearing neatly pressed summer-weight wool pants, a button-down shirt and his loafers. What happened to his golf attire? He looked like he had just taken a shower; his hair was slightly damp and combed back from his forehead.

"What's this?" she asked, pointing to the flowers. "Meeting George for dinner?"

Dan grimaced. "I'm sorry, Beth," he said. "I'm so sorry about lunch. I should have left the guys and met you at noon like I promised." He pushed the flowers toward her. She took them silently. Dan stepped closer and kissed her on the lips. She didn't kiss him back.

"And I'm sorry about George, about him harassing you last night. And me grilling you. I should have trusted you."

Maybe not, she thought, turning away. It was Jake's kiss, not Dan's that burned on her lips.

"I got the job," she said quietly.

"Great!" Beth jumped as Dan's voice went from a near whisper to a shout. "Congratulations! We have to celebrate!"

When she didn't look back at him, he walked around to face her.

"Aren't you happy?" He kissed her again and backed up. He looked confused at her cold response. "Well, you should get cleaned up, and we'll go to dinner. You must be famished. I'll call in a reservation."

Beth shook herself out of her funk. Yes, dinner would be good, given that she had no lunch. "Nothing fancy," she said straight-faced. "Let's just stay here, eat at the restaurant. I don't feel like going out."

"Okay. That's fine," Dan said, walking her to the elevator. "You're doing your last lesson tomorrow, right? You should rest up tonight. And maybe we should leave early. Get back to Seattle? Maybe Friday instead of Saturday? You'll want time to get ready. And I'm going to be swamped at work when we get back."

"Right," she said flatly. "I'm skipping the last lesson.

Maybe we should play tomorrow, just the two of us. Let's see if this trip was worthwhile. But without George. And then let's leave on Friday."

"Sure!" It sounded like he was missing her clues entirely. She wasn't excited about dinner or golf or leaving. Nothing seemed to matter right then.

As the elevator door opened, he let her walk in alone. "You clean up, and I'll go to the clubhouse to get us a tee time for the morning. What time you want to meet for dinner? 6:30?"

"Sure, whatever." The elevator doors closed, and Beth rode up, her face buried in the roses.

By the time Beth's salad arrived at their table in the dining room of the hotel that night, she had already consumed two full flutes of champagne and was starting to regain her sense of humor. What had she been thinking? That she and Jake would live together in Palm Springs—a place where a big, shaggy dog like ChiChi could never be comfortable—working on her golf game? How would she keep him away from the next good-looking beginner who graced his practice tees?

Yes, his kiss was seductive. He was seductive. He acted like he understood her, but what did he know about her life? What did he understand about her love for dogs and Seattle rain and strong coffee and good Columbia Valley wines? Not much. And yet, here she had been fantasizing about … well, she wasn't really sure what the brief fantasy had been, but at least it had been brief. She could be proud of that.

"I'm sorry about this afternoon," she said. She tried to look contrite. Was it working?

Dan looked confused. "Sorry about what? I was the one who was late for lunch."

"No, I mean I'm sorry about not being more grateful

for the roses, for pouting. I should have been happy about the job. I don't know where my head was."

Dan nodded, probably pleased about being let off the hook for missing their lunch date. Her contrition was a relief. "You're probably tired," he said. "It's hard playing golf every day. Even I get tired. Maybe we should take the day off tomorrow. Sit by the pool?"

"No, we need to play," she said. "I need to see if I really learned anything, or if I just looked better because we were playing a scramble."

"You mean you and Jake?"

"Yeah." She shook her head. Her and Jake. That wasn't going to be such a thing as "her and Jake" anymore. "And we won't be able to play in the sun again for months."

"Rain, rain, and more rain," Dan said. "What are we going back for?"

Beth blinked. She was actually looking forward to going back. First, there was ChiChi. She needed to bury her face in the big dog's furry back and soak up some unconditional love. Second, she was a bored with the unchanging weather in the desert. The same dry, sunny day over and over. She liked Seattle's rain. Or drizzle. Or whatever it is. On the other hand, would Seattle's rainy winter cause her to lose whatever golf skills she's picked up over the past week?

"When do your new clubs arrive?" Dan asked.

"Ten days, they said," she said. "I hope they don't rust before I get a chance to use them."

"But you'll be busy with the new job," he said. "Time flies. Before you know it, we'll be furiously planning our wedding."

That word "wedding" stopped Beth cold. Oh, that! She knew Jake wasn't part of her future, but did that mean she had now accepted as fate that she was marrying Dan?

As if to answer her unspoken question, Dan stood up

and dug in his pants pocket. Immediately, she knew what he was doing.

"Oh, no," she uttered under her breath.

Dan knelt next to her chair and held out a diamond ring. "I've waited too long to give you this. You've already said you'd marry me. But will you say it again?"

Beth looked at the ring. It was pretty. The diamond wasn't as ostentatious as it could have been, given Dan's salary. And it was set in a wide, platinum band with just enough filigree to be interesting. She looked at it sadly.

It was time.

She nodded.

"What?" Dan said, egging her on.

"Yes, I will marry you."

Dan stood up and put his hand out. She laid her palm on his, and he slipped the ring on her finger. As he sat back down, Beth glanced out toward the patio. Jake sat watching them. He twirled his Scotch on the rocks and held up the glass to toast what he'd just seen.

She quickly looked away.

Fifteen

BETH BRUSHED HER TEETH, WASHED her face, and kicked off her shoes. Barefoot, she pulled open the sliding door to her room's balcony and stepped out with the phone to her ear.

"This is Ellen," her mother answered her call.

"Hi, Mom. It's me."

Just then a motorcycle started up in the parking lot below, and Beth stepped back inside and closed the door. She sat down on the bed, staring at the mountains in the distance.

"Beth? What is that noise? Where are you?"

"Sorry, Mom. I was out on the balcony and a Harley just started up."

"Oh. Your father and I were just talking about you, wondering how the lessons are going."

"Oh, fine," Beth said. "But I'm calling to tell you I'm coming home early. I can pick ChiChi up Friday afternoon.

I got the job at Starbucks. I'm anxious to get home and get ready. I start on Monday already."

"Congratulations, dear," her mom said. "I am happy for you. Are you excited?"

"Yes, I am."

"But do you have to pick up ChiChi? Maybe she'd like to stay with me this weekend."

Beth laughed. "I know you'll miss her. But you will have plenty of babysitting opportunities once I go to work. ChiChi will probably see you more than she'll see me."

Her mother proceeded to tell her a half-dozen ChiChi stories. How she'd chased a squirrel who was now visiting her every day, sitting on the fence to chatter insults at her. How she wouldn't let Beth's father sit on the sofa, having decided it belongs to dog and mom only. And more. Beth listened patiently. She missed the furry dog enough that even her mother's long-winded tales couldn't bore her.

"Well, lots to talk about, Mom," she said, finally cutting off the narratives. "I'll see you day after tomorrow."

Beth lay back on the bed and stared at the ceiling. Telling her mother about the new job was easy. What she'd avoided telling her was the news she was less likely to take well—the formal engagement. The ring. The promise to plan a November wedding. Ellen wasn't fond of Dan in the first place, and now that she and ChiChi had bonded so, it was unlikely she was going to like him as a dog-averse son-in-law.

Beth raised her left hand and looked at the ring. It was attractive. It was tasteful, although probably expensive. She could do worse than Dan. Stable, wealthy, healthy Dan. She tried to think back to when she fell in love with him—or at least when she had convinced herself she had. But she couldn't put her finger on any kind of turning point that represented "falling" in love. Somehow the idea that she loved him had taken over her mind and body like some low-impact chronic disease that wasn't necessarily difficult or unpleasant but was impossible to purge. Did she really think it was that bad? A chronic disease? She remembered telling Jake it was like a bad habit.

She thought about her friend Deb's relationship with Jason. It wasn't always smooth, from what Deb told her. But it seemed passionate, mulit-layered, intriguing. Maybe that's how all relationships looked from the outside. Maybe on the inside, they were all either tempestuous or boring.

Would it be the same with Jake? The charge she got out of being next to him—and that kiss!—was more powerful than anything she could remember experiencing with Dan. Or had she forgotten? Had Dan once thrilled her the way Jake did? She tried to remember Dan's first kiss. It had slipped her mind.

Weary from the rollercoaster of the day's emotions, Beth scooted off the bed and pulled off her dress. She threw it over the easy chair in the corner and slipped under the covers. She reached up to switch off the lamp next to the bed and lay back on the pile of pillows. She held her hand up and looked at the gleam of the diamond in the pale light from the parking lot.

Probably, she thought, she'd feel less conflicted about marrying Dan in the morning. Perhaps a round of golf together would be just what she needed to put Jake out of her mind and remember why she agreed to marry Dan in the first place. And if that didn't work, at least back in Seattle, she'd have ChiChi and a job. Whatever happened, she'd be okay. Better than okay. She'd be just fine.

The sun was just about to rise above the clubhouse behind them when Dan teed off the next morning with Beth watching. The air was crisp and the mountains to the west were pink from the early, angled rays. Beth imagined this could be her first great day of golf with Dan, ever.

Of course, that was too much to expect.

She had just walked to her tee box, set her ball, and taken a practice swing when she felt Dan's heavy presence, already judging, already critical. Taking a deep breath, she tried to ignore him and lined up for her shot. Immediately Dan yelled. She turned, and he ran up to her holding his hands in the air.

"Stop. Stop!" he yelled. "Honey, stop. You are standing too far from the ball. Didn't Jake show you this?"

He stood behind her and pushed her closer to the ball.

"There. That's better. Go ahead." He backed away.

Beth took another deep breath and tried to shake off her irritation. She lowered her shoulders like Jake had told her, but her arms were stiff, her hands too tight, and the ball never left the ground. It skittered about thirty feet, not even reaching the fairway.

She picked up her tee and stomped to the cart. "I wish you'd just let me play. I am not out here to get a lesson. I just want to play golf. Okay?" She threw her club into the bag and pulled out a smaller fairway wood. She strode forward to hit her second shot.

Dan pulled the cart up beside her. "Okay. But you're never going to enjoy the game if you don't have the right basics. And your setup on the tee box is one of the basics."

She tried to block out his voice, took her swing, and hit a fairly decent shot. Not great, but not as bad as the first one.

As they worked their way to the first green, she tried to relax. She watched how Dan took his practice swings, set up to the ball, and swung the club. Perhaps if she could garner something helpful from his example, she could rescue the day.

On the green, Dan putted first. Beth watched him sink the ball from about twenty feet. "Great putt, Dan. It looks like all that practice you had this week didn't hurt," she said.

She stepped up to her ball and lined up for her putt. She stroked, and the ball just slipped past the hole. It wasn't a bad shot. Just not a one-putt.

"You looked up," Dan scolded.

She glared at him. "What?"

"You looked up at the hole before you were finished with the stroke. That will always push the ball right for a right-handed golfer. Didn't Jake teach you anything?"

Disgusted, Beth picked her ball up. She slammed the putter back in her bag and sat in the cart.

"Aren't you going to putt out?" Dan asked. "You can't keep your score if you don't putt."

She waited until he got in the cart before answering.

"I'll say it once and not again. This is not a lesson. And I don't care about keeping score. Just leave me alone and let me play. Okay?"

Dan threw his hands in the air, surrendering, and drove to the next tee box. "Okay, I just want us to have fun when we play golf together, and you'll have a lot more fun if you stop making these mistakes."

"To you, they're mistakes," she said. "To me, it's just a shot. I can't imagine what our honeymoon golf trip will be like."

"Well, you've got a year to practice," Dan said, proving how clueless he was. "But I don't think I'll pay for any more lessons from Jake."

"Would you just drop it?" They'd finished only one hole and already Beth was angry. "Drop the Jake thing? Jake and are nothing to each other. Never were. There's only room for two people in this cart. No room for Jake. No room for George. Okay?"

Dan shook his head like he didn't understand her anger. "Okay. I'm sorry. I'll drop it." He stopped the cart, grabbed his driver, and walked up to the tee. "It's just that you two just looked awfully buddy-buddy at lunch," he said quietly, as if he wasn't sure he should say it out loud.

"What do you mean? What lunch?" Beth asked. Then she remembered. She remembered Dan and his new buddies watching them from just off the patio the day she and Jake went shopping for clubs.

"You mean Sunday? It looked like you were spying on me."

"No, we just happened to walk by when you two were on the patio."

"So that's why you didn't want me to have lunch with him again."

Dan stood with his club in his hands. "What was going on between you two?"

Beth didn't know if she should waste her breath answering. He had clearly already formed his own answer.

"We became friends," she said. "That's all. And I'll never see him again, so I don't know why this continues to bug you so much."

"It bugs me because—"

She cut him off. "You said you'd drop it!"

"Okay. Yes. I will," he said, turning to line up his drive. "Let's see if we can just forget it and enjoy the beautiful day."

"Yes. Let's." But by this time, only on the second of eighteen holes, Beth knew it was a lost cause.

Pulling up to the cart barn after the eighteenth hole, Dan was figuring out their scores as he drove.

"Want to know what you got?" he asked. It was the first word either of them had said to the other in more than two hours.

"No thanks. I really don't." She shook her head and got out of the cart, pulling off her glove and putting her ball back in the bag.

Dan smiled broadly and waved the scorecard at her.

"Boy that week of golf really improved my game. I'm going to have to reconsider how much I'm working when we get back. Maybe I should find a little more time for golf."

He hopped out of the cart and chatted with the attendant who came over to clean their clubs. Beth walked away, heading for the hotel.

"Hey, wait up," he said. "I'll just arrange for them to bring our bags up. What do you want to do for lunch?"

"How about nothing," she said under her breath. She straightened up and turned to him. "I'd like to just grab a sandwich at the cantina and go to my room. I have to pack, and I'm really exhausted. Then I think I'll finally have that drink at the pool. Alone."

"Okay, I'm going to take a nap. How about dinner?"

"We have a seven o'clock flight in the morning. Do you mind if I just order room service and go to bed early?"

"No," he said, his eyebrows knit with confusion. He walked up to her. "I suppose that's fine. I'm sorry our vacation is ending on such a bad note. Maybe when we get home, we can talk things over and get back on track."

So, he did notice. He may not have minded their total lack of communication over sixteen holes, but now he finally seemed to realize they had a problem.

"Yes," she said. "We will have to do that."

Sixteen

Beth changed into her swimming suit, determined to wear it at least once on this "vacation," and headed for the pool. She doubted she'd even get in the water. All she wanted was to sit by the pool and drink until she fell asleep in the warm desert sun.

She threw her towel on a lounge chair, kicked off her flip-flops, and walked to the edge of the pool. She sat with her feet in the water. A waiter took her drink order, and Beth leaned back with her hands on the concrete behind her and turned her face to the sun. This, she thought, was what she probably should have been doing the past six days. It would have been much better preparation for taking a new job on Monday. Better than what she'd done: Falling for her golf instructor. Fighting with Dan. Wasting money on a set of custom golf clubs.

Was that what she had done? Did she fall for Jake? Or was it just a vacation infatuation? When would she know which it was? As she played with Dan that morning, Jake was constantly on her mind. But that didn't prove anything. And it had been so long since she'd had a real crush on a man, she wasn't sure how serious to take it.

The waiter delivered her drink, and Beth stood up and stretched out on her lounge chair. Three drinks later, she put the back of the seat down and let herself fall asleep, her face in the shade of a big deck umbrella, her legs warmed by the late fall rays.

It was midafternoon when Beth left the pool and started packing for the trip home. She nibbled on a sandwich and while she folded up her golf clothes, she worked on a single-serving bottle of pinot grigio she had bought in the gift shop. She was nearly finished packing—as much as she could be before brushing her teeth again in the morning.

With her wine glass in hand, she opened the slider to her balcony and stepped out. Down on the driving range below, Jake was finishing a lesson with his new customers—a couple of women. She watched as he stepped up behind one of them with his arms alongside of hers and their hands together on the club. It was just as she remembered. She shook her head, disgusted with herself, and walked back inside.

The flight to Seattle was full, and Beth should have been happy to have a first-class ticket. The seat was comfortable, she had a bottomless mimosa, and the novel she had brought with her was engaging. But she was sitting next to Dan, who was focusing on the view out the window. She didn't feel happy.

They had just become formally engaged after nearly a year of an informal betrothal, and overnight she had become intolerant of him. It wasn't because his behavior had changed. It was her attitude. Perhaps the ring was the cause—was she now at the point of no return? By accepting it, her mouth had committed to something her heart had not. Yet. Perhaps it would once they were back to their normal lives and the idea sank in.

The plane climbed above a cloud layer over Pasadena on the far side of the San Jacinto Mountains from Palm Springs, and Dan turned away from the view to her.

"What did you do for dinner last night?" he asked.

'Room service." Beth tried to put some warmth into her voice. All morning, her responses had been mostly monosyllabic and cold.

"Good?"

"Just a sandwich. The wine helped."

"Did you put it on the room?"

"Yes. Was that alright?" For the first time on the vacation, she wondered if she should have been paying for some things. She didn't have any money, but she had credit cards, and soon she'd be making a nice salary. "I can pay you back. I can pay you back for this whole trip. Just give me a couple of months to get caught up on bills."

"Not necessary," he said, smiling and reaching for her hand.

"Well, I'm quite sure you don't think you got your money's worth from those golf lessons," she said. She considered saying she was sorry, but she wasn't sure what she'd be apologizing for. She'd tried. She'd made progress. It just wasn't apparent when she played with Dan. And for that, he needed to apologize; she didn't.

"It doesn't matter," he said. And he returned his gaze to the clouds out the window.

BETH WAS EXHAUSTED BY THE time she retrieved her car from her apartment garage and drove to her mother's house to get ChiChi. But seeing the big dog run to her with such joy gave her a temporary shot of adrenaline. She dropped to her knees and tried to hug the wiggling malamute, who twirled in and out of her arms as if she couldn't decide where she wanted to be scratched first.

Ellen stood over them watching. "You'd think she was mistreated while you were gone."

"You're probably tired of sitting up on that old couch with Grandma, aren't you little girl?" Beth asked ChiChi in her doggie-talk voice. "That Grandma is so mean!"

Finally, the tangle of fur, legs, and tail settled down, and Beth stood up. She followed her mother to the kitchen with ChiChi at her heels.

"Coffee?" Her mother held up the carafe from the old Mr. Coffee she'd been using for years.

"Sure," Beth said. "I could use a pick-me-up."

Her mother reached in the cabinet for the coffee can and filters, and Beth changed her mind. "Could you make it decaf. I didn't get much sleep last night. I need to go to bed early."

Her mother lifted an eyebrow suspiciously. "Not much sleep?"

Beth laughed. "It wasn't what you're probably thinking. No, Dan never saw the inside of my room nor I his."

"Well, why didn't you sleep? Didn't you have fun?"

Beth considered her answer as she watched her mother measure out the coffee and fill the maker with water.

"I had fun. But Dan and I tried to play a round together yesterday, and that was anything but fun."

"Then, when was it fun?"

"The lessons were fun," Beth said, spreading her hand out and looking at her ring again. "I had a great time with Jake. He was the best part of the trip."

Her mother pointed at the ring. "You mean that wasn't the best part?"

Beth shook her head, exasperated. "I don't even know why I accepted this." She sighed and felt her body sag. "But maybe now that we're back home, things will settle back down. Maybe Dan and I can get close again."

"You know, that's what vacations are supposed to do for you—bring couples together. You get away from all the worries back home and focus on each other. I'm sorry it didn't happen."

Beth was surprised her mother was saying anything vaguely sympathetic about her relationship with Dan. She'd never liked him, but maybe the ring had changed things for her mother, too—just in the opposite direction.

"I'm afraid Dan was more focused on his two new golfing buddies than he was on me," Beth said.

"And you, my dear. What were you focused on?" Her mother looked at her with soft eyes.

"Oh, it's not important, Mom. I'm sure I'm not the first girl to fall for her golf instructor."

Her mother rounded the bar and put an arm over Beth's shoulder. "Well, you'd better figure things out before next November. If this"—she pointed at the ring again—"is a mistake, it's better to know it sooner than later."

Seventeen

⚑

GETTING HOME DIDN'T HELP, AFTER all. Settling down and getting into a regular routine still didn't bring Beth any closer to feeling sanguine—let alone happy—about her official engagement. But the new job distracted her most of the time and kept her from panicking over her sense that her relationship with Dan was crumbling a little more every time they got together.

"Not hungry?" Dan asked her at dinner a couple of weeks after she had started working at Starbucks. Beth shrugged and pushed the green beans on her plate into straight lines.

"More tired than hungry," she answered.

"Do you like the new job?" Dan asked.

"So far." Beth quit trying to eat and pushed her plastic Lean Cuisine plate across the kitchen bar. Each day at work she was being thrown into more projects, learning the Starbucks way of doing things along the way. She expected it would take a few more weeks before she felt fully comfortable there.

"I mean, what do you know about a job at first?" she said. "Really? It's not much different from my last job except that there's a lot of pomp and circumstance about 'team'—you know, 'team player,' doing it 'for the team,' and such. No one is an employee. Everyone is an 'associate.' Kind of kitschy, I think."

Dan nodded. "It takes a while to settle in, get the feel for a new culture." He'd been patient with her refusal to see him more than twice a week while she was adjusting to the new job. Beth appreciated that.

She stood up to rinse her plate off in the sink before shoving it in the near-full garbage can. Dan got up and did the same. He stretched and looked across the bar into the living room, where ChiChi had made herself comfortable on Beth's couch. After her stay at Ellen's house, the dog had decided there were new rules, and she liked them.

"Hey, dog! Get off the couch!" Dan yelled.

ChiChi lifted her head and looked blankly at him. Then she slowly laid her big jaw back down between her front paws and closed her eyes.

"Her name is ChiChi, not 'dog,'" Beth said. "And I don't think she's going to listen to you. Not after a week with Mom."

Dan shook his head, disgusted. "Oh, well, I'm sure she'll be adopted soon now that you're back to take care of it."

Beth hesitated. She hadn't broken the news to him yet—the news that she had adopted ChiChi before they left for Palm Springs. She wiped the bar down with a sponge and dried her hands on a paper towel. She took a deep breath.

"Uh. Actually, Dan," she started, sitting back down on the barstool. "I have to tell you something."

Dan turned to her with a look that indicated he knew

he wasn't going to like this.

"What?"

"I adopted ChiChi a week before we left for Palm Springs. She's my dog now."

Dan threw up his hands. "I thought we had an agreement. No more dogs."

"It was less of an agreement than a unilateral decision," Beth said, surprised she could sound so calm and rational. "I never agreed."

"Yes, you did. I'm sure you did."

"Dan," she said, "sometimes you assume people are going along with you just because they quit arguing."

"Oh, really? Like when?"

Beth swallowed. It was time to admit her ambivalence about their engagement. "Like when you decided we were getting married. You never really asked. You just assumed."

"Didn't you say yes in Palm Springs?"

"Yes, but that was long after you—"

Dan cut in. "And now you don't know?"

Beth had no answer. Dan waited for one, even though her silence probably spoke louder than her words would have. When was she going to be strong enough, brave enough, honest enough to accept her mistake and put her voice to it?

Dan waited for her answer, but she sat mute. He slammed his palms on the counter, eliciting a growl from ChiChi, and stomped to the front door. He pulled his rain jacket off the hook.

"I don't know what more to say, Beth. Why don't you think about this for a couple of days? We need to figure this out before we make any more plans."

He slipped on his jacket, and then hesitated, as if he was waiting for her to call him back. When she didn't, he gave her one last glance and opened the door.

"Goodnight," he said, and disappeared.

Beth rose from the stool and plopped down on the couch next to ChiChi. The dog moved her head over onto Beth's lap and closed her eyes again. Beth scratched her ears affectionately. "He didn't even say goodnight to you, did he?"

BETH WAS VAGUELY AWARE OF someone standing in the doorway of her office, but her mind was elsewhere. It wasn't until Deb's voice rose to a near shout before she shook herself out of her reverie and paid attention.

"What?" she said.

"Do you want to join me for lunch?"

Beth shook her head. "Nah. I'm not hungry. Go on without me."

Instead, Debra walked in and sat down in the chair in front of Beth's desk. She twisted and lowered her head to try to catch Beth's downturned eye.

"Okay. 'fess up, sister. What's going on?"

Beth shrugged. She didn't feel like talking, afraid that even opening her mouth to speak would unlock the floodgates to the tears she was holding back.

Beth continued, all business. "You don't seem like you're really here. If you want to keep this job, you've got to get into the team spirit. You've got to start acting like you want to be part of the team."

Beth lost her battle with the tears, turned her head to look out the window, and tried to wipe her eyes without Deb noticing.

"I just don't know what I'm doing here," she said. She pointed at the rain. "Look at that."

"At what? It always rains here in the winter."

"I'm quite aware of that," Beth said with a bit of unintended snark. "I've lived here all my life."

Deb said nothing for a long minute, and finally Beth looked back at her.

"I have a feeling this has something to do with that golf instructor," Deb said, a crooked smile on her face. "It's really not the weather, is it?"

Beth shook her head and smiled, embarrassed at the truth. "Yes," she said. "It's the weather."

Deb chuckled and held her eyes.

"Okay, no," Beth said.

Deb's voice softened. "Is he thinking about you?"

"I don't know." She didn't really want to talk about Jake with anyone. She was afraid it would extend his presence in her mind. Already she was frustrated by how many weeks she'd thought about him, long after she should have gotten over her schoolgirl crush.

"What do you know?" Deb wasn't giving up.

"Well." Beth hesitated, but continued. "Dan sent me an email he got from Jake thanking him for taking lessons. It had Jake's phone number attached."

"So?"

"So he and Dan didn't exactly hit it off. Dan didn't even last a day in the lessons. There was no reason for Jake to send that email to him—no reason unless he was hoping I'd get his number that way. I don't think Dan understands that or he wouldn't have forwarded it to me. But clearly, Jake is leaving it up to me to call him—if I want to. After all, I was the one who walked away that last day with nothing to say."

Deb nodded and pursed her lips. She stood, picked up Beth's cell phone from her desk, and handed it to her.

"Here," she said. "Only one way to find out."

Beth took the phone and stared at it as if she weren't quite sure how to use it. She looked up at Deb. "Right," she said. "Why don't I make a phone call and meet you down at lunch in a few?"

Beth waited until Deb was out of earshot, and still she couldn't bring herself to select Jake's number she'd taken off of his email to Dan and stored in her phone. She imagined Jake standing in the bright sunshine of mid-day on the driving range, an eager young woman hanging on his words, watching his beautiful swing. She didn't realize she'd actually dialed the number until he answered.

"Hello?"

"Jake?"

"Beth?" Did he recognize her voice, or was he guessing only she would be calling him from a 206 area code?

"Hi ... Jake." She hadn't practiced what to say, and now she stumbled for words. "Are you busy right now?"

"Uh." Jake apparently hadn't practiced what to say if she called, either. "Uh, Beth? Um." He paused again, but then his voice strengthened, and he sounded more like himself. "I'm giving a lesson. But I can take a minute. I'm surprised. What's up?"

"I have two questions for you. Okay?"

He paused. "Okay."

"Well, the first is sort of silly. Or I should say I'm a little embarrassed to ask it. But what really happened with you and George's girlfriend?"

Jake chuckled and Beth could imagine his smile as he formed his answer. "Well, it's simple. I know Dan will probably never believe it. George certainly never did. This is it: She was furious with George and thought she'd get even by coming on to me. I'll have to admit it kind of worked. At first. But once I figured out what was going on, I ran as far away from her as I could. By then, she'd lost interest in both of us. Me and George."

"Oh." Beth let that information soak in.

"Good answer?"

"As long as it's true."

Jake laughed. "Of course it is."

Beth was surprised he took that personal question so well. If it weren't true, could he have answered so easily?

"What's the second question?" he asked, trepidation back in his voice.

"Oh, this is easier," she said. "Do you like dogs?"

Eighteen

Beth waited for Dan at a booth next to the window at a seafood restaurant on the waterfront and watched the gulls swoop up and down over the pier. She had a hard time imagining living anywhere but Seattle, where the wide bays of Puget Sound dominated the views west, the great peak of Mount Rainier punctuated the view south, and the Cascade Range lined the horizon to the east. Palm Springs had been a nice, warm, sunny break in the otherwise drizzly and gray winter, but it wasn't home.

Jake had responded enthusiastically to the pictures of ChiChi she had sent to his cellphone, and they had fallen into a routine of swapping short text messages about the weather, work, and ChiChi. Their exchanges were platonic and trivial; apparently neither of them wanted to venture into anything more personal or revelatory. But it was a start, Beth thought. It was friendship. And didn't all true loves start that way? As friends first?

She wasn't sure she wanted more than friendship with Jake, especially if they continued to live this far from each other. But even a long-distance, platonic relationship was more satisfying than her relationship with Dan these days. Dan no longer seemed as much hurt as disappointed by what had happened to them.

And now it was time to stop disappointing him and get off the fence.

Dan spotted her from the hostess desk and waved meekly. She was surprised again—like she had been in Palm Springs—at how his confident, authoritative personality seemed to evaporate around her these days. He walked across the restaurant, his worried look indicating he knew why she'd asked him there.

"You wanted to talk?" he said, standing next to the booth.

"Yeah. Join me?"

Dan shrugged off his raincoat and slid into the booth across from her. "Why do I have a bad feeling about this?" he asked.

"Look," she said. She smiled wearily. "We both know we have to do this. It's not easy, but it's time."

Dan looked out the window at the gulls and the water and the shores of West Seattle in the distance. "Is this about Jake?"

"Kind of," Beth admitted. "But not in the way you think. I'm not in love with him."

"Yet," Dan added for her. The scene outside held his stare.

"Yes. Yet," she said. "Jake helped me realize that there are others out there, men I might have more of a connection with. And maybe with Jake it will grow into something more. But, really, Dan. It's not about Jake. It's really about us."

He refused to meet her eyes. Could a man so strong

and successful in business be so ill-equipped for affairs of the heart? If he was hurt, he couldn't admit it. He couldn't fight for her. Maybe he'd never invested much of his heart in her. Maybe it was just another item on his "grown-up" checklist that he needed to complete: Get married, have kids. Anyone would do.

She slipped off the ring and held it out to him in her open palm. He glanced at it and finally looked her in the eye.

"I guess it's been obvious for some time. But that doesn't make it easy."

"I know," she agreed. "But we've spent a lot of time together, and it just isn't working. I think trying to play golf together was a great idea. It showed us that the problem wasn't just a lack of mutual interests."

"Is it the dog thing?"

"It's not that simple either. It's not one thing."

A waiter approached their booth, and Dan waved him away. "No," he said. "You're right." He returned his gaze to the window. "I guess this is it, then?"

She nodded, holding the ring in her outstretched hand. "I know you really want marriage, a family. But you have to find the right person. Not just anyone. Not just the woman you picked up by the hamburgers and baked beans at a picnic."

Dan smiled at her description, perhaps at the memory.

"So, yeah. This is it." He picked the ring out of her palm and twirled it in his fingers.

"Yeah. It is."

Neither of them said anything for a long minute. Then Beth picked up the menu lying in front of her. "But as long as you're here, how about some fish and chips?"

"So it's just for the weekend?" Deb asked Beth as they stood together at the window in Beth's office, staring out at the rain. "You're going to fly down there and back and be at work on Monday? Is that even possible?"

"It's only a two-hour flight," Beth said. "And I have to know. It's the only way to figure this out. Text messages about the weather aren't telling me what I need to know."

"Haven't you talked about this at all? No phone calls? Just texts? Seems like not much to go on."

Beth turned from the window and turned off her computer. "Exactly. I can't keep trying to figure out what I feel from 1,200 miles away. I have to walk up to him, face him, and see if there's a there there."

"So to speak," Deb said, laughing. She turned from the window too, pulled Beth's raincoat off the hook behind the door, and handed it to her.

"Well, I hope figuring it out doesn't mean you'll leave us."

"I know. I like this job. And I complain about the rain, but I would miss Seattle. It's home. Do you know there are no decent fish and chips in Palm Springs?"

Deb looked at her watch. "Well, you'd better run if you're going to catch your flight. Want me to walk you out? Make sure you don't chicken out?"

"Oh, if I needed that you'd have to come all the way to the airport with me and shove me on the plane. No, I know I have to do this. I will do this."

"Well, good luck. I'll see you Monday morning, whatever happens, right?" Deb leaned in and gave Beth a quick hug.

"Right," Beth said, walking out the door. "Close up my office for me, will you?"

It was January, so it was already dark outside as Beth pulled her rollerbag out the heavy front door of the building and jerked the hood of her coat up over her hair. Her head down, fumbling with her purse, her suitcase, and her car keys, she walked into someone.

"Oh, I'm sorry!" She pushed the fabric away from her eyes and looked up.

"Jake?"

He stood before her, flashing his big, beautiful grin. "In the flesh. Fancy meeting you here!"

"I work here! What are you doing here?"

Jake took the handle of her rollerbag and put a hand under her elbow. He led her back under the overhang at the door of the building.

"Remember that golf school I wanted to start?" he said.

Beth didn't know what to say. Seeing Jake right there in a dark, rainy afternoon in Seattle was too confusing. It made no sense.

"Well, funny thing ... " Jake paused. Out of the rain, Beth could now study his face. She had thought she'd have time on the plane to Palm Springs to plan what to say to him and how to control her emotions when she saw him. But now that he was right in front of her, she couldn't think. Now she faced a rush of feelings she wasn't ready for.

"What?" she asked. She sounded as frantic as she felt. "What's going on?"

Jake put his hands on her shoulders as if to calm her down. "Remember when I told you about that guy I played with on the tour who grew up here?"

"Yeah." She thought she did.

"Well, he and his dad own a golf course south of town. They've got a big warehouse next to the course. They want to start an indoor, year-round golf school there. I came up to check it out. Maybe I can start my golf school there."

Beth took a deep breath and tried to clear her head. Seeing him was such a shock she had trouble concentrating on what he was saying.

"But that's not all of it," he continued.

"Uh-huh?"

"I know you were unsure about how you felt about us

weeks ago in Palm Springs. One minute I thought we were growing close, and then you'd pull away," he said. "But I wasn't confused. I knew how I felt. I felt it that first afternoon on the driving range. Even with Dan right there."

So it was about more than a golf school, Beth realized. This was about her. About them.

"But coming here," she said. "This is a big risk. What made you so sure?"

"I've been sure for a long time—since that call when you called to ask me if I liked dogs. It took me a while to arrange things and quit my job, but I took a chance that you asked for a good reason. Am I right? Was that a test?"

Beth laughed and nodded.

"So," Jake said, "I thought as long as I'm here checking out the golf school thing, maybe I should come by and check out my intuition." He glanced at her suitcase. "But I see you're headed somewhere?"

Beth shrugged. "I was. I'll bet you'll never guess where."

He squinted as if thinking hard. "Palm Springs?"

"Good guess."

He stepped forward, his eyes focusing on her lips. She reached for the lapels of his raincoat.

"I didn't know you owned one of these," she said.

He pulled her close and pressed his lips against hers. She melted into them, just as she had in Palm Springs. His kiss was the same, but this time, she didn't quit. She could give in.

Finally, they separated, and she took a half step back, looking into his eyes, her heart pounding in her ears.

His eyes were soft. Maybe, she thought through the rush of emotion, what they had between them was stronger than she had been daring enough to hope for. And maybe she didn't have to move to Palm Springs to have it.

"Know what sealed the deal for me?" he asked.

"My golf swing?" she guessed.

"Nope," he grinned. "Guess again."

She shook her head. She had no cogent thoughts, just a craving for more of his lips.

"ChiChi," he said. "Once I saw those pictures you sent, I knew I had to meet her."

Beth was amused. "ChiChi doesn't always have that effect on people. But I had a feeling..."

His kiss told her she didn't have to say any more.

Author's Note

I STARTED WRITING THESE NOVELLAS as screenplays about a month into the Covid-19 quarantine. I had passed the time that first month watching Hallmark Channel movies—something I had never done before. I found the films calming and mind-numbing in a good way. The formula was easy enough to parse, and Hallmark's guidelines are laid out clearly on its website: no violence and no sex. From watching, it was clear that swearing, religion, and politics were off-limits as well. Once I finished the screenplays, I turned them into these novellas. I imagine the readers most likely to enjoy this book will be those who enjoy Hallmark's romantic films. But even if you've never watched one in your life, I hope you find these stories calming and fun to read.

About the Author

Marjorie Pinkerton Miller* is the romance pen name for Marj Charlier, author of nine contemporary and historical novels, two romance novels, and three romance novellas. Her first historical novel, *The Rebel Nun*, was published by Blackstone Publishing and won first-place prizes for historical fiction and overall fiction in the 2023 Colorado Independent Book Publishers Association EVVY awards. A former *Wall Street Journal* reporter, she holds degrees in journalism from Iowa State University and the University of Wisconsin-Madison, and an MBA from Regis University. She lives and works in Colorado Springs, CO, with her husband, the journalist Ben Miller.

*Pinkerton was the author's paternal grandmother's maiden name, and Miller was her mother's maiden name. Marjorie is her given name.

www.ingramcontent.com/pod-product-compliance
Lightning Source LLC
Chambersburg PA
CBHW021555310726

48972CB00003B/837